RESNOVAS

*Something
Someone*

"You will know the truth, and the truth will set you free." -John 8:32

This is a work of fiction. Names, characters, places, and incidents either are the product of the author's imagination or are used fictitiously. Any resemblance to actual persons living or dead, events, or locales, is entirely coincidental.

Copyright © 2023 T.G. Scott

All rights reserved. No part of this book may be reproduced without prior permission of the author.

Cover Design by: T.G. Scott

RESNOVAS | II

someone
T.G. Scott

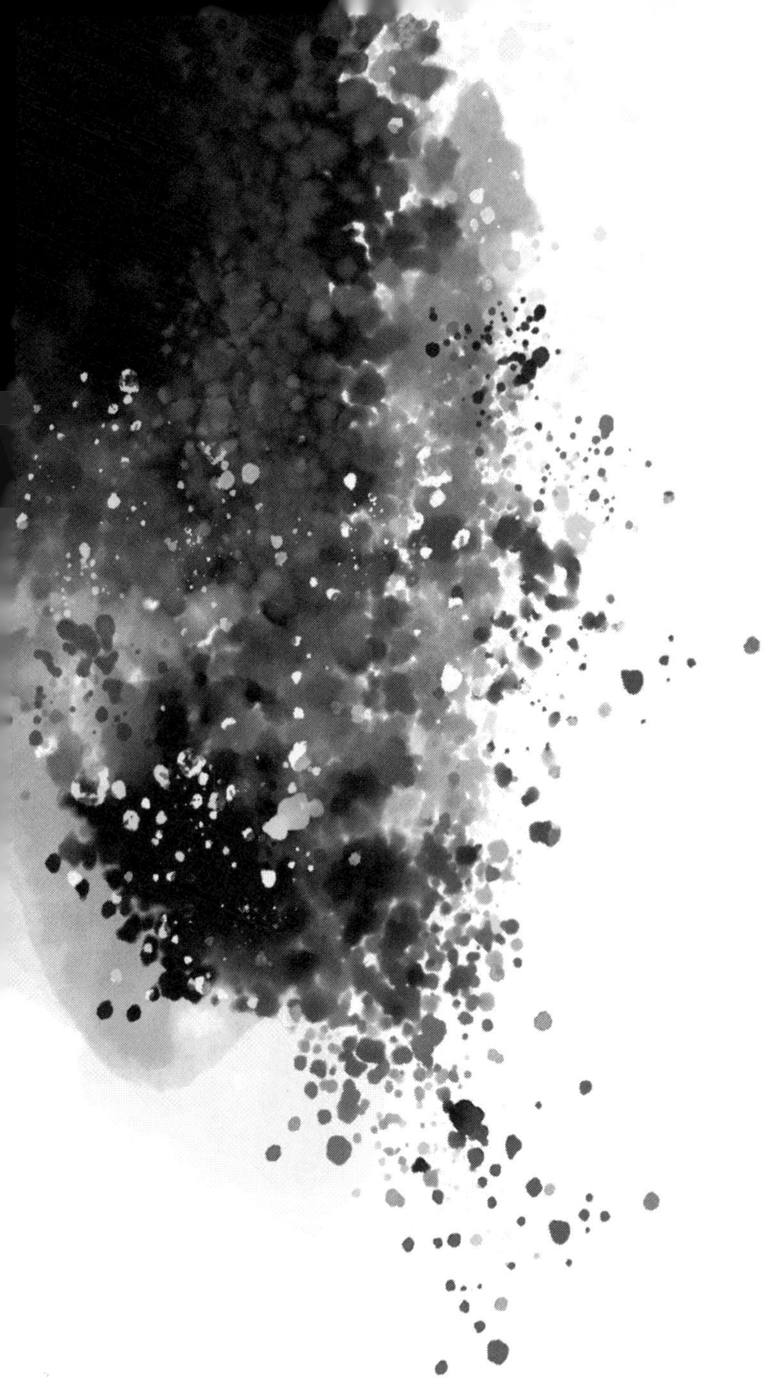

someone

I

Wade Walker strode down the streets of Birch, his amber eyes scanning the dusty town with a look of weary disinterest; it was a Wednesday, early, and the kind of oppressive hot that made one imagine he could almost smell brimstone.

Wade could imagine pretty well. The reminder of where his soul was *not* headed did him some good, and he pulled off his sable cattleman. He fanned his sweat-plastered, sandy brown shock with it.

The few people on the street eyed him as he walked by. The townspeople usually kept away, not quite shunning him but certainly not welcoming him either. He wasn't concerned with their lack of hospitality. The only problem was that it made it hard for him to get work, therefore hard for him to get food.

And therefore, he was heading out of town into the nearby woods to hunt. It wasn't easy to shoot a squirrel or rabbit with his old six-shooter, but he always made do. He was almost to the town's "Welcome to Birch" sign when he heard shouting somewhere nearby. He stopped, straightened, and glanced around. Someone crashed into him from behind, nearly knocking him off his feet.

Stumbling back, he lashed out with one hand while drawing his revolver with the other. A girl with wild hair and even wilder eyes jumped back, holding her hands up. She was a little thing, wearing a long white shirt which reached her knees. Her legs were inappropriately bare, and she had no shoes.

She glanced over her shoulder as Wade lowered his gun. Two figures were whooping and running that way. One, he saw, held a stick, and the other had a rock.

"Get back here, you little freak!"

someone

Wade whipped off his long coat and threw it over the kid's shoulders.

"Come on," he said, motioning. "This way."

She looked back at her pursuers, then at Wade. She seemed to decide he was safer and followed him. He set her in the shadow of a tall building, pushing her down to the ground and pulling the coat over her head. He stood beside her, facing the outside, pistol drawn but held low at his side. The two young men passed by, oblivious. When they had gone, he knelt beside the girl.

"Hey you," he said. "Why're they chasing you?"

"I don't know," she answered, pulling the coat off of her head and looking up at him. She looked about as bewildered as he felt.

Something cool and circular pressed against the back of Wade's neck.

"Turn around," said a voice behind him.

The girl looked past Wade and scrunched her nose.

"I told you to back off!" she snarled.

Wade whipped around, shoving the guy's gun-holding hand and fixing his own revolver on him. Both assailants were young, not yet twenty, Wade reckoned. Couple of donogooders, probably the sort who threw rocks at birds to get their kicks. The first one had that particular gleam in his eyes; this was not the first time he'd done something like this. Wade felt concerned for any childhood pets the boy might have had.

"Git!" Wade hollered. "I'll shoot the both of you."

The second one backed away, but the first remained where he was, sneering.

"Why are you doing this?" Wade asked.

"Reckon she's the crazy girl from Oak they say went missing," he said, brandishing the weapon in his hand. "They're looking for her, maybe we can get something out of it. Thought we'd learn her some *sense* before we haul her back."

"Don't you know who *he* is?" said the second boy, wringing his hands. He'd dropped the rock a long time ago.

"Should I?" the first one asked.

"Last chance," Wade said.

The young man smirked, cocked his pistol, and said, "You won't do squat."

someone

Wade fired, taking off the toe of the boy's boot, along with the appendage. He screamed and clutched at his nubby foot, saw the remains of the dismembered toe, vomited. Wade whistled.

"You've got yourself a problem there, boy," he said. "You better go get that looked at real quick."

The boy shuffled backward. He made it to his feet and hobbled off, howling. His friend reemerged and helped him along toward the town's infirmary. Wade turned back to the girl, who stared at the mess on the ground, unfazed.

"I didn't think you were gonna do it," she said, nodding. She looked up at him. "Honestly."

She reached out her hand. Wade started to take it, realized she was left-handed, and quickly switched hands. She'd already switched to her right also. They repeated that whole process once more before figuring out the handshake.

"I'm Quinn," she said.

"You got a boy name?" he said.

She squinted. "No."

Wade gave her a funny look, but did not say anything

else about it.

"Well, I'm Wade," he said. "Walker. Alright then. Um, you got a home or something?"

She shook her head.

"Where's your parents?" he asked.

"Got none," she said. "Maybe in the real world. But-"

"What?" Wade interjected. "What're you talking about, the real world? This is the real world."

"No," Quinn said. She looked like she'd told this story a million times before. "This isn't the real world. That's what I've been trying to tell people forever and ever. Nothing is real. None of this. It's all…Ah, I don't know. But it's not real."

She's confused, Wade thought. *Real confused.*

"Look, missy," Wade said, kneeling and scooping dirt off the ground. He took her hand and let the dirt pour from his into hers. "It's real. That mess on the ground's all real too, but I reckon you don't want to touch that."

"Yes, I know," she said, exasperation tinting her voice. "But it's still not…this place is still not real."

Poor kid.

Wade stood.

"Why aren't you wearing...proper clothes?" he asked.

"I don't...I don't know," she said, rubbing her forehead, a troubled look crossing her face. "I can't remember."

Wade shrugged, twisting the band of metal on his left fourth finger. He glanced down at it, studying the braided texture. He never could remember where it had come from, just that he'd been wearing it a long time.

He turned his eyes back to the girl. The sun was rising steadily toward noon, and activity was increasing in town. The mercantile was open.

"Well, come on," he said. "Let's go find you some."

Wade led Quinn around the building and into the street. He looked over his shoulder toward the infirmary. There was a trail of blood headed that way. Hopefully those two young men would be busy for a long time in there.

When they reached the mercantile, he opened the door for the girl, holding it as she went inside. She still wore his big coat, which dragged on the floor, so at least she was somewhat covered up. He nodded at the man behind the counter. The man did not return the gesture, only stared.

Wade walked to the back, where he knew there to be clothing. There. A nice dress. She'd look right pretty in that pink color, if you could get over that wild brown hair of hers.

Before he could suggest the pink dress, she had already picked out a pair of boy's trousers and a baby blue button-down shirt. She walked into the back and came out a couple minutes later, wearing those clothes.

"You can't wear that," he said.

"I am not wearing one of those, if that's what you mean," she said, tilting her head at the dresses.

Wade crossed his arms.

"What are you, some sort of suffragette?" he asked.

"I don't know what that is," Quinn answered.

The trousers were much too big for her, and she selected a belt. She tucked her shirt into the pants, and put on the belt. She found socks and boots, then pulled a long jacket off the shelf, like his, but smaller and lighter in color.

Now that she had some actual clothing on, he could see she was older than he had originally thought- probably seventeen or eighteen, as opposed to his previous conjecture of fourteen.

someone

He swiped a little tan hat from a cubby and shoved it on her head, the rim falling down over her eyes.

"All set, now that you've emptied my wallet?" he asked.

She pushed up the hat's rim and nodded. She was more annoying than he'd previously conjectured, too- but maybe that was because she was older. He rolled his eyes and they walked to the counter. He paid, and they got out of there as quickly as he could shove her out the door.

"You hungry?" he asked the girl.

She nodded, the hat bobbing on her head. He waved for her to follow him, and they walked to the town's café.

After he got her some breakfast, Wade still had not figured out what to do with her. Who would take this girlchild off his hands?

"Missy Quinn," he said, as they walked away from the café. "You sure you don't have a home somewhere?"

She shook her head.

"No," she said. "I was trying to tell you..."

"Yeah, I know what you were trying to tell me," he interrupted.

Did somebody knock her on the head real hard, or was

she just this way anyhow? How confusing it must be to believe that the world is not real. Just then, he spotted a lady he sort of knew: Catherine, an inn-owner.

"Miss Catherine!" he shouted, waving her down.

It took three shouts for her to pay attention to him.

"Yes, Mr. Walker?" she said, finally.

She was a large woman, with wide shoulders and big hips; trim, but sturdy.

"Would you take this young'un?" he asked. "I'm not quite sure what to do with her."

The lady hissed to him, "She looks a little wild."

"I heard that!" Quinn stated, eying the inn owner with contempt.

Catherine frowned, thought, and finally nodded.

"I need some help at my inn. But if she gives me trouble I'm throwin' her out," she said.

"I reckon she'll be alright," Wade reassured.

Catherine shrugged and took Quinn by the forearm roughly.

"Wait!" the girl said.

Catherine frowned and yanked her arm. Quinn looked

at Wade pleadingly. He averted his eyes. Catherine quickly jerked her again, and Wade had second thoughts. But she was better off with Catherine than with him. He had done what he could- saved her from those boys, clothed her and fed her.

She would be safe there with Catherine; if not from whatever was going on in her head, then at least from real things like men and starvation and the elements. He went home to his shack-of-a-house outside of town thinking these things, a feeling of unease taking root in the back of his mind as he walked.

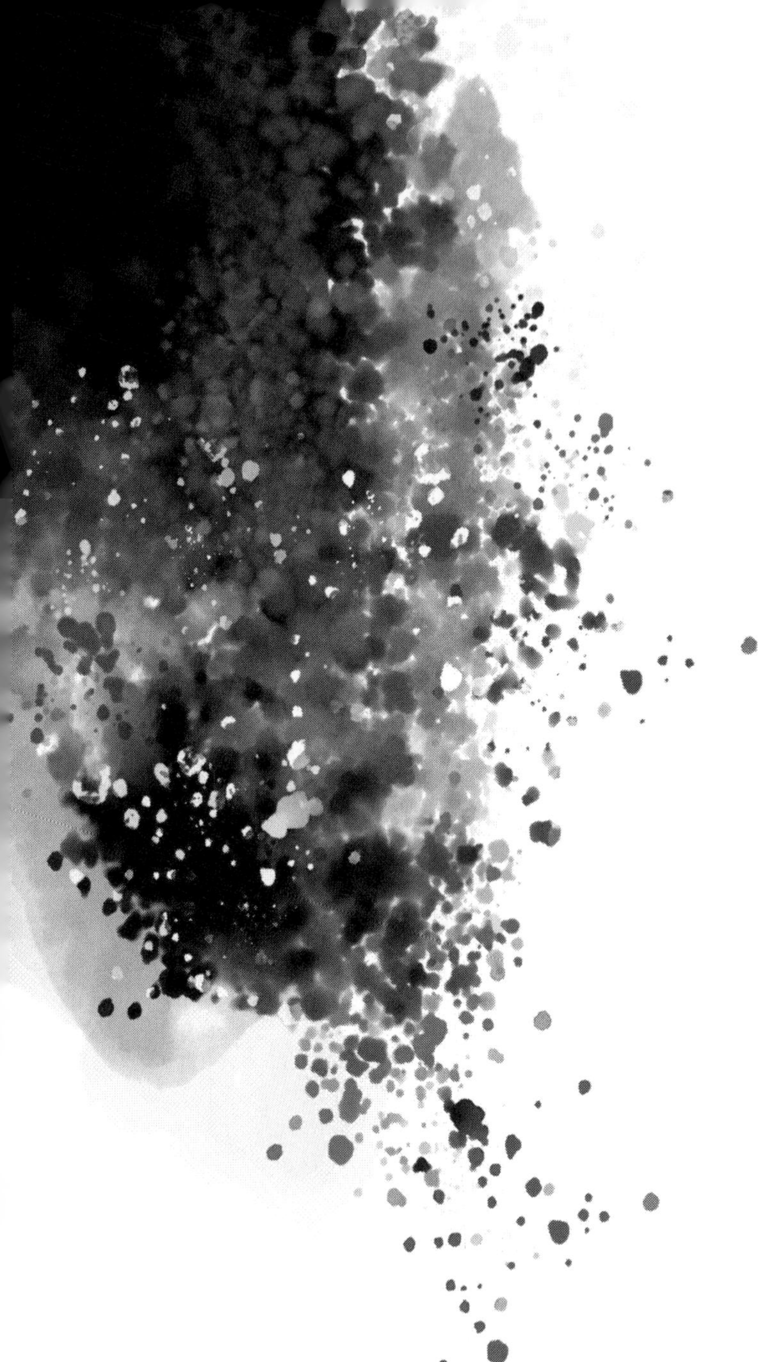

someone

II

Quinn sat at Catherine's kitchen table, frowning. The woman looked her over.

"What happened?" Catherine asked.

"He saved me," she said. "Two guys were chasing me. Wanted to beat me up."

Catherine hmphed. "How come you got boy clothes on? You'd be a looker if you'd dress properly."

"Because you can't do anything in a dress," Quinn answered.

Catherine eyed her for a few moments.

"Where you come from?" she asked.

"Well, I reckon we must all come from the real world,"

Quinn said.

"What?" Catherine interrupted. "Who filled your head with that muck?"

"No one!" Quinn said. "This is not real. It's-"

A sharp pang shot through her head, and stayed there, setting the backs of her eyes on fire and cancelling her thoughts and speech.

"What's wrong with you?" Catherine spat. She smacked Quinn on the side of the head. "I am talking to you!"

"My head..." Quinn squeaked.

"Come on, get up," Catherine said, pulling her to her feet.

The motion vexed her further, and she found herself on the ground.

"Fine, you just stay there," Catherine said, after trying to get her to her feet. "You really are crazy. What have I gotten myself into?"

Quinn peeled her eyes open in time to see the woman walking away.

What have I gotten myself into? she thought, before blacking out.

someone

The fierce pain in her head had cleared out by the afternoon. As soon as she was back on her feet, Catherine put her to work. Catherine had turned her home into a small inn, with four rooms for people to stay in. Currently there were two tenants, but the unoccupied rooms had been left filthy by their previous owners. It had taken the rest of the day to clean them.

Now Quinn lay on a little floor cot in the kitchen, thinking. She wished the Walker guy had not passed her off so fast. She liked him, and somehow he seemed vaguely familiar to her.

If only someone would believe her... Sometimes she came close to believing the people who called her crazy. After all, no one else knew.

The real world was Terra.

She did not know what Terra was, but she knew it was real and this was not. She was not sure Terra was better than here, but she wanted to find out. Something was off in her head, or something was off in everyone else's. They could not both be right.

And there was yesterday, which she did not remember.

Today she had awakened in the street, wearing that odd, short gown, completely disoriented; she didn't even know what town she was in. Then the two guys were chasing her, and then she found Wade. She thought back to the days earlier. What had she been doing?

She ran away from the orphanage on Monday, the day before yesterday. She had spent her entire life there, as far back as she could remember, to the age of six. Twelve years later, she still could not recall anything prior to her arrival at that place.

On Monday, she had been climbing a hill to get a view of where she was heading. She had been wearing her red shirt, with a split skirt and her own trousers. She had spotted people, and started going the opposite direction. Her memory blanked, and the next thing she remembered was standing in the street this morning, Wednesday, a whole day later. Tuesday was entirely lost to her.

Quinn knew what she needed to do now: she was going back to that hill. Her orphanage was in the town of Oak. The hill was right outside of Oak.

Oak Hill.

someone

She recalled it being described as haunted and being warned not to go up there. She never had, until Monday.

What was this town called? She would ask Catherine in the morning, and find out how far it was to Oak. Then she would return to Oak Hill and try to figure out what happened yesterday. Now that she had a plan, she managed to fall asleep.

The subsequent morning, Quinn was fed breakfast, and then put to work scrubbing the kitchen down. At noon, one of the tenants left, and she cleaned his room. She stripped the bed, changed the sheets, swept and then mopped the floor, and dusted.

Catherine was then screaming for her to come down and help cook dinner. Quinn never got a chance to ask the woman her questions, and soon found herself in her cot for the night once more.

The next morning, before Catherine could tell her what to do, Quinn posed her question, "What town is this?"

"You mean to say you don't know what town you're in?" she said.

Quinn shook her head.

"Birch," Catherine said.

Another tree name. Quinn cupped her hand around her chin.

"How far to Oak?" she asked.

"That where you're from? No wonder you're so dang crazy," Catherine said, to which Quinn frowned. "My old beau used to live there. Said it was too far from here to there, and stopped comin' to see me."

That's definitely why he stopped coming to see you, Quinn thought.

"How do you get there?" she said.

"Eh, just follow the main road out past the 'Welcome to Birch' sign. Maybe. I don't know," Catherine said.

Quinn nodded.

"Now get! That second tenant left, and there's another one supposed to be here right after breakfast. Get movin'!"

Quinn got moving, and plotting. After she cleaned the empty room, she snuck back into the kitchen and snooped around in the pantry some. She found a pack, some jerky, a red bandana, and a canteen. Deeming the canteen too bulky, she left it for later, taking the other items and hiding them under the cot.

She looked in some of the drawers around the room, finding a hook and some fishing line. She spotted a high cabinet. She would have to climb on the counter to reach it.

After quickly checking to see if anyone was around, she scaled the counter and opened up the cabinet. Inside she found an old but shiny six-shooter, with a holster and one box of spare bullets. It was too bulky to hide under the cot, but she would come back for it when she retrieved the canteen. Just as she jumped off the counter, Catherine came bustling in.

"What're you doing, girl?" she demanded.

Quinn, feigning a vacant look, pursed her lips and looked all around. Finally she set her eyes on Catherine. She might as well use her supposed insanity to her advantage.

"Huh?" she said.

Catherine shook her head, then crossed the kitchen to the stove. A plate of eggs from yesterday sat there.

"Take those up to the new tenant in her room," she ordered.

"Alright," Quinn said.

Catherine fixed her eyes on the cot for a moment, tilting her head to view it from different angles. Quinn held her breath. Finally, Catherine shook her head and exited the kitchen. Quinn walked over to the counter and studied the eggs. She picked a little bit off and tasted it. Bad.

Feeling spiteful toward Catherine for serving her patrons disgusting old food, she went outside, around the house, to where a small chicken coop was. She grabbed two of the eggs and took them inside.

Such rebellion.

She threw the old ones out the window and fried the fresh ones over the stove, rinsing out and returning the pan to the cabinet so the woman would not know the difference. She slapped them on a plate just like the other and took it upstairs to the now-occupied room. She knocked.

The tenant answered the door and took the plate without even looking at her.

Which was good. Because Quinn knew that woman. She was Ava Mark, one of the heads of the orphanage where Quinn had lived. The woman must be here to find her. She someone had to leave tonight.

Darkness fell. Quinn lay in bed for four hours. She counted to sixty, sixty times, and then did so four more times; fourteen thousand and four hundred seconds. Then she rose. She re-braided her hair and shoved it up into her hat, then fastened the bandana around her neck in case she needed to cover her face.

Quinn pulled out the pack, and retrieved the canteen from the pantry. Then she climbed the counter and took that six-shooter, its holster, and the box of bullets. She loaded the revolver quickly before fastening the holster to the rear of her belt, sliding the gun into it, and putting the bullet box in her bag. After doing one last search of the pantry, she snuck out the door. She filled the canteen at Catherine's well, and headed for the main road.

All was dark and silent, until she passed by the saloon. She pulled her hat down over her eyes, buttoned her coat up over her chest, and hurried by. Just as she made it past, she heard scuffling. A young man limped out of the building, shoving a girl out with him. He demanded that she hand over her purse. Quinn recognized him as one of her pursuers: the vile-tempered, violent one now missing a toe.

"Stop!" the blonde girl squeaked.

Debating, deciding to go on, and then turning back around, Quinn pulled the bandana over her nose.

Deepening her voice, she shouted, "You!"

He ceased his attack briefly, then resumed.

"Stop!" Quinn yelled.

He glanced over his shoulder, then turned all the way around, one hand up, one holding onto the girl.

"Calm down," he said, then muttered something about "money" Quinn couldn't quite hear.

Anger rising in her chest, Quinn said, "Let her go."

He raised his brows challengingly.

"What're you gonna do, midget?" he said.

She whipped the revolver out, dropped it, but just as quickly had it refixed on him. He laughed.

"I don't think you know how to use that thing," he said.

The blonde tried to make a break for it, but he held her fast.

Quinn knew how to use the gun. She used to have a revolver much like this one that she would take far into the woods to practice shooting. She was a good shot, though she doubted she could take someone's toe off like Wade had. Ava Mark had discovered the gun and thrown it into the pond on orphanage property not long ago. Quinn dove for it numerous times, but had never found it.

"Come on," said the guy, voice rising hysterically, hands groping for the purse. "Hand it over!"

The blonde struggled against him, but couldn't break out of his grip. He took a large knife out of his pocket, bringing it to rest against the girl's throat; Quinn saw a trail of red trickle down her neck.

Quinn pulled back the hammer. He stopped at the click and narrowed his eyes, malice replacing the smirky arrogance.

In a sudden move, he shoved the blonde girl aside and drew a fat pistol from somewhere on his person, firing at Quinn twice, missing both times. She stumbled backward, tripping in the gravel, barely hanging on to her gun.

He stalked toward her, making a show of being unencumbered by his injury.

"Wait a minute..." he said, studying her. "You ain't

a midget! You're just that crazy girl…" He looked at the cowering blonde and screamed at her, "Go on! Got what I need now." She skittered away, clutching her small bag to her chest.

He took aim, fired again, closer to hitting Quinn this time; she fired back, also missing as her head swam in panic.

"Wonder if they'll pay me for your body."

His lips pulled back over his teeth as he closed the distance between them.

"What're you going to do, little girl?" he said, enjoying watching her squirm. "Who's going to save you now?"

Anger steadied her. He aimed again, but she was faster- this time her shot found its mark.

Bang.

He hollered out an obscene name and collapsed as she sprinted off. Quinn ran as fast as she could, searching for the "Welcome to Birch" sign Catherine had mentioned. She heard shouts behind her.

There! She ran past the sign, turned off the road, and made for some trees. It was a thick wood, good for hiding in. She heard water, and headed for that sound. She crashed through the brush, not bothering with covering her tracks, until she came upon the origin of the noise: a stream.

She slid her boots and socks off and put them in her pack, rolled up her pants, and stepped in. The water was cool but not freezing, which felt pretty good on a hot night such as this. Now she no longer had to worry about her trail. She walked upstream. Once she was certain that no one was tracking her, she would find the road.

Quinn realized she had not reloaded yet, and fished the ammo box out of her pack. She quickly slipped bullets into the cylinder's two empty spaces, then holstered the revolver. She attempted to slow her breathing, but adrenaline would not allow it.

She wondered if the boy she shot would die. A heavy feeling settled in her chest. She didn't believe she had done the wrong thing -he would have killed her and the other girl- but that did not lessen the weight of it.

Quinn kept moving through the night. The water she sloshed through seemed to get heavier and heavier. How far away from town was she? Were they tracking her already or would they let her go? Probably not. They would want to apprehend her, and doubtless send her back to Oak with Ava Mark.

What have I gotten myself into? she thought again.

Perhaps it was good that she was heading for Oak. Who would expect her to go there? Then again, she was supposed to be crazy, so why wouldn't she? She decided to go with the former supposition.

She walked through the stream for a while longer before finally deciding to take a break. She found a spot where leaves had piled up and stepped there, so she would not leave footprints. She grasped the branch of a nearby oak tree, and pulled herself up. From there she kept climbing until she was nearly at the top.

The next day, at what she judged to be around four in the morning, Quinn descended from her tree and continued her upstream trek. She came to a small pool where she spotted a couple of fish.

She sat on a rock on the little shore and pulled the hook and fishing line out of her pack. She dug around for a bit,

someone

found some worms, and baited her hook. She cast it out and waited.

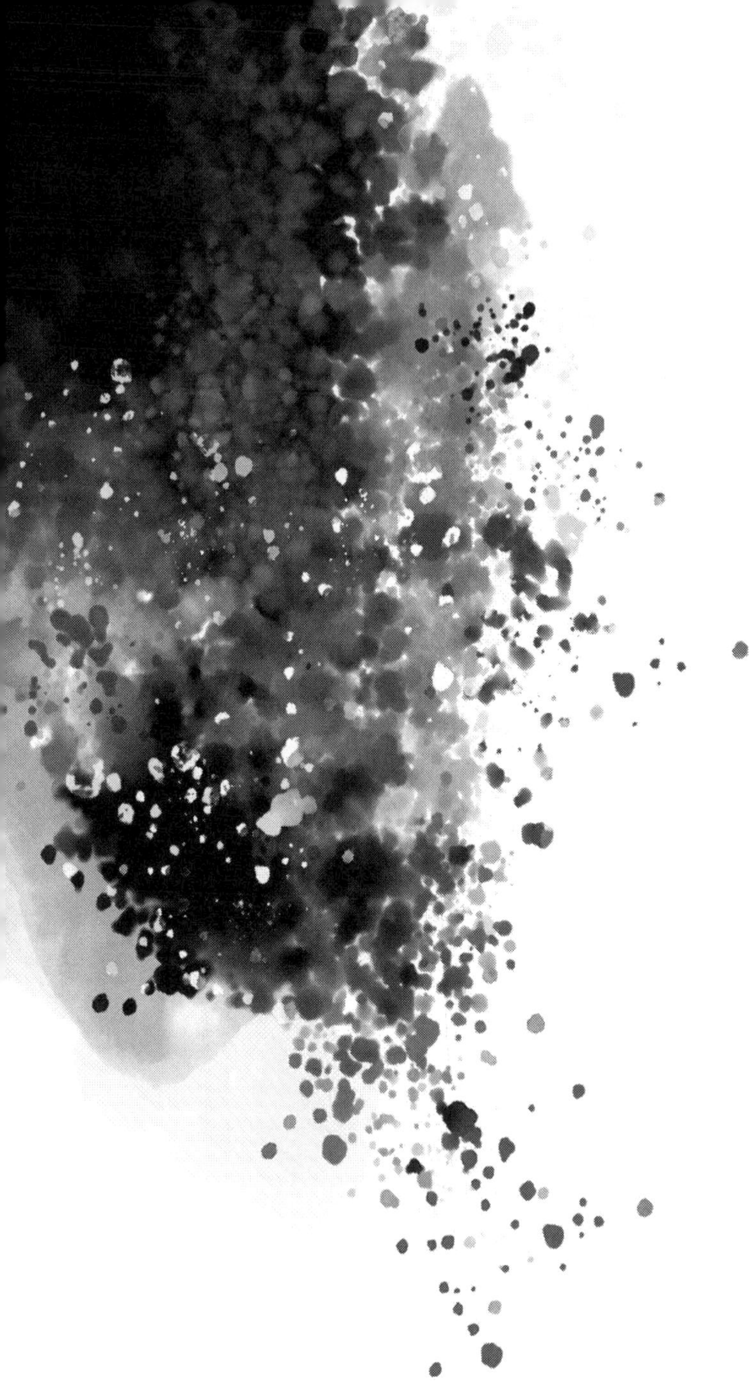

III

Wade tramped through the woods outside of Birch. He was tracking the girl, Quinn. The night before, the town's bartender had come knocking at his door. Wade, wearing nary but his underwear, had thrown on his long coat like a robe and answered the door.

"A boy's been shot outside the saloon," the man had said.

Wade raised his brows.

"Shot by a girl," the bartender continued; he had a squawky voice, like a high-pitched lady-parrot, that got on Wade's nerves. "A girl who Catherine at the hotel states you forced her to take in."

One of Wade's brows lowered while the other remained aloft, and his lips stayed unmoving.

"Catherine says that she isn't dealing with it. So that leaves you. The boy seems to be pulling through, but if he doesn't, we've got a murderess at large. A murderess tied to you. And given your reputation as the *former* lawman of Hickory..."

Wade scowled.

"I'll find her," he said.

The man mumbled something about where Wade ought to go when he died.

"No, I don't think I will," Wade responded.

He closed the door. He got dressed, packed a bag, readied his revolver, and locked the door behind him as he left. First, he had gone to see Catherine.

"Mornin', Miss Catherine," he said when she answered her door. She frowned.

"Come on in," she said.

He followed Catherine inside; they each took a seat at her kitchen table. A cot was made up in one corner of the room, and a stool stood before a high, open cabinet. Wade looked at Catherine, waiting for her to speak.

"That girl you gave me robbed me, ran off and shot a young man last night," she said. "Turns out she's some violent runaway from the next town."

Wade pursed his lips.

"I'm taking responsibility for her," he said. "I'm gonna track her down, and figure out what happened."

Catherine nodded.

"Don't think there's much to it," she said. "She's insane. Tried to kill one of our boys. What more do you need to know?"

She stood and gestured for him to leave.

"What did she take?" he asked as he got to his feet.

She pointed to the open cabinet.

"My old revolver and its bullets, a bag, a canteen. Maybe more. Not sure yet," she explained.

Wade had left Catherine's hotel and walked over to the saloon. There he noted several bullet holes in the ground, and boot scuffs in the dirt, the size of the pair he'd bought just the other day. He found a waitress who told him which way the girl had run: outside of town, into the woods.

"He was going to kill her," the waitress told him quietly, as they stood apart from the other people swarming the scene. "Something about her dead body for money. They had a regular shootout."

He'd followed the girl's tracks to a stream, where they stopped. He reasoned that she would not follow the water down, back toward Birch, so he followed it the other way.

And now here he was, following the water upstream and uphill, piecing together an idea of what happened. The boy with the sadistic streak had gone after her again, and this time she'd had the means to protect herself. The townspeople were making her out to be the menace, but from what Wade gathered, her actions had been in self-defense.

He heard quiet splashing. He slowed his pace, drew his gun, and cocked it. The splashing ceased; he kept walking, coming to a small pool. There beside it he saw something reflect light: the line of a makeshift fishing pole, stuck into the shore on one end, awaiting a fish.

He scanned the muddy shore. There. Boot prints, scuffling away toward the trees. They matched the ones in the street outside the saloon.

someone

Click.

She was somewhere around here, she had a gun, and he could not see her. He did not like it. He turned in a circle. He saw something move in a tree- a bird. Something clattered on the ground behind him, and he whirled around.

The girl was just standing after retrieving her gun from the ground. They both stood still, weapons trained on each other. The makeshift fishing pole pulled out of the ground, having hooked something. Quinn did not take her eyes off of Wade.

"You gonna get that?" he asked.

"No," she said.

"Why did you shoot that boy?"

"You shot him too."

Him. He'd been correct in his assumption about the boy's identity. Wade studied her eyes, reading unease in their blue.

"He was attacking another girl outside the saloon. I told him to leave her alone. Then he came after me." She flipped the gun in her hand, holding it out to him. "Here, take it." Her eyes remained intently on his as he accepted the revolver. Wade holstered his own gun and un-cocked hers.

"I believe you," he said.

"You do?"

"Yeah." He nodded. "The evidence lines up. If I was still...if I was sheriff there, I'd have arrested him long ago. Should've taken his gun from him, too."

He returned the revolver to her. She holstered it, nodding her thanks.

Quinn asked, "Is he dead?"

"They told me he seemed to be pulling through," Wade said. "But that could've changed since."

She dipped her chin and walked to the bank of the stream. Her fishing pole had caught on a root, and she crouched near the water, grabbed the stick and pulled in the line.

She retrieved a pack from a bush nearby, tossing the line and stick inside. She stood, turned, nodded at him, and began walking away upstream, apparently no longer concerned with her tracks.

Wade stood there for a moment, then said, "Missy Quinn?"

someone

She stopped and spun on her heel, looking at him expectantly.

"Where're you going?"

"To find out the truth."

"About what?"

She hesitated. "About whether or not I'm crazy."

Wade chewed his lip. She ought not go off by herself- but ought he follow her? He grunted finally and started walking after her. Someone had to make sure she was alright.

She veered away from the stream, toward the road. Wade kept following. Once they had reached the road, Quinn stopped and turned.

"Don't you have something better to do?" she asked.

"As a matter of fact, I do not," he answered.

"Huh," she said. "I thought you were some kind of lawman."

He shook his head with a grim look on his face, and she did not push that subject any further. She began walking again.

"So where're we going?" he asked.

After being silent for a few minutes, she said, "Oak."

Hadn't she run away from Oak? There was an orphanage there, he knew. Was that where she'd come from? Why on earth had she run away, only to go back? But he did not ask. If he asked too many questions, she would shut down completely and answer nothing. Probably run off and disappear.

The sun was getting ever higher, and the temperature with it. No clouds drifted through the sky, and no wind blew. Two hours passed, and Wade could see the other town up ahead. Quinn stopped and looked on. Wade stood beside her and glanced down. She was frowning, thinking. She crossed her arms over her chest, tapped her top lip. Then she started walking again.

When they were several yards from the entrance Quinn veered off to the right, walking around the rickety buildings. Wade could see several people going about their business within. Would they recognize the girl if they saw her?

Quinn started for a big hill perhaps three miles away. Fifteen more minutes of walking later, Wade detected the sound of a horse approaching. A lone rider was heading for them from the direction of town. Quinn turned and looked, then pulled her red bandana over her nose, tipped her hat down over her eyes, and hurried her pace. Wade followed close behind.

"Hey!" shouted the man on the horse. "Stop!"

Quinn kept going, so Wade kept going.

"Who's that?" he asked.

"Sheriff of Oak," she answered.

Bang!

A shot sizzled the ground near Wade's foot. He and Quinn both halted promptly.

"I said *stop*!" said the sheriff.

They turned. Sweat glistened on the man's suntanned skin. His hat was slightly askew, and his badge flashed in the sunlight, stinging Wade's eyes. In one hand, he held a long, beautiful rifle; the other hand clutched the reins. He looked a few years older than Quinn, with a pleasant face. The young man squinted past a pair of round glasses. Recognition dawned on his face, and his eyes softened.

"Quinn? Is that you?" he said.

Quinn defeatedly lowered her bandana.

"Hey, Andy," she mumbled.

"Where've you been?" he asked, smiling good-naturedly. "Ma and Missy miss you."

"I miss them too, Andy," Quinn said.

"Since you gone and disappeared, everyone's been...well, I've been looking for you. And that old hag Missus Mark been looking for you. She went all the way down to Birch!" the young man, Andy, said. "Hasn't returned yet, thank the Lord!"

"I saw her," Quinn said.

Her demeanor held back something. Hostility? Distrust? Irritation? All three? The two stood, looking at each other. Andy coughed.

"Well, I suppose you can lower your hands now. Who's this?" he said.

Wade and Quinn lowered their hands, and she said, "This is Wade."

Andy dipped his chin in greeting and slid off of his horse. She was a pretty horse, strong, with a tan coat and a neatly brushed white mane and tail. She was well taken care of and healthy. Andy slid his rifle into a saddle holster.

"Where're you going, Quinn?" Andy asked.

She crossed her arms and shrugged. Andy looked like he was going to say one thing, then changed his mind and said something else.

"Come on," he said, motioning. "Won't you come see Ma?"

Quinn looked up at Wade. He shrugged.

"Alright," she said. "Just for a while."

Andy turned the horse around, and rather than mount her he walked a little ahead of them.

"Who's he?" Wade asked.

"Andy," Quinn said.

"Who's Ma?"

"Andy's ma."

Wade sighed. She was as reserved as he was -when she wasn't spouting her "not the real world" nonsense- and he was beginning to find it annoying. Was he annoying because of his reservation too?

The sun had reached its pinnacle now, beating down on the earth mercilessly. As they approached, Quinn pulled the bandana over her nose again. Andy noted this, Wade saw, but said nothing.

They entered Oak. It appeared to be a nicer town than Birch. The buildings, though old and worn, were better maintained, and the people had slightly nicer clothing.

"Where do you come from, Wade?" asked Andy as they made their way through the town, garnering curious looks from the people around them.

"A town about, eh, thirty miles out, that way," he said, gesturing loosely to the right.

Andy nodded. He stopped in front of what looked like the sheriff's office, and bid them go up the steps while he took his horse around back. The spacious porch had five wicker chairs positioned on it, and a single pot held a yellow snapdragon.

"What are we doing here?" Wade asked.

"I don't know," Quinn said, looking at the floor.

Andy returned a few minutes later, smiling an oblong grin. What did Quinn have against him? Wade wasn't one to make quick judgements about people, but the young sheriff Andy seemed alright.

Andy pulled a key from his pocket and unlocked the door, then held it open for them as they went inside. It was

someone

warm in there, but not blistering as it was outside. To the left Wade saw two barred jail cells, ahead a door with a sign reading "Sheriff," and to the right a flight of stairs.

"I'm gonna go tell her you're here," Andy said, going to the stairs. "Just...wait there."

He ascended quietly. Overhead, Wade could hear soft voices, a gasp, and a louder one. Andy returned to the top of the stairs.

"Come on up, Quinn," he said.

She walked up the stairs and followed Andy into the space above. Wade paced around, twisting the band on his finger, trying to listen. Soft voices again. But nothing he could understand.

Presently Andy came back, followed by Quinn and a redhaired young lady, who was helping an elderly woman down the stairs. Quinn smiled and talked quietly with the old woman, who despite her age was very beautiful. Andy paused at the bottom of the stairs and helped the pretty old lady down. He guided her to the door and outside, where he helped her into one of the wicker chairs. Wade, Quinn, and the redhead followed them out. She offered her hand to Wade.

"I'm Missy," she introduced herself; she had a soft, pretty voice to match her soft and pretty features. "Mrs. Connor."

Sheriff Andy's wife.

"Wade Walker," he replied, shaking her hand.

The old woman suddenly gasped. "I forgot to get tea for everyone!"

She attempted to get up out of her chair, but Missy made her stay, going in to get some herself.

The woman smiled a little and said, "Such a good girl." She looked up at Wade. "I'm sorry, sir. I'm afraid I don't know your name. Please, tell me, what is it?"

He tipped his hat. "Wade Walker, ma'am," he said. "And you?"

She blushed.

"Oh, me? I'm Allie Connor," she said, then turned to Quinn. "Where've you been, girl? Going off and leavin' us to deal with that mean old witch Ava Mark."

"I know, Ma, I'm sorry," Quinn said, taking the woman's wrinkled hand. "I didn't mean to. I got sort of lost."

someone

"You? Lost?" Allie said incredulously.

"I know," Quinn said. "But it's true. I wound up in a whole other town. Mr. Walker helped me get back."

"That so?" Allie said, beaming at Wade. "My, he be handsome *and* kind?"

She fanned herself. Wade fidgeted. Quinn grinned a little. Missy finally returned with tea. She passed it around and then perched on the arm of her husband's chair.

The conversation drifted to the drinks, with Allie giving her daughter-in-law some critiques. That lasted five minutes, as it took the old woman quite a while to make all her points. Then she turned back to Quinn.

"You turn eighteen yet, girl?" she asked.

Quinn nodded. "I've been eighteen, Ma. But in the orphanage record they've got my birthday wrong. So according to them, I'm still seventeen, and they won't let me leave."

"Seems you can if you want," Andy said, pointedly.

Quinn smiled, but it faded away quickly.

"I can and I am," she said. "I've got to go."

"Where?" Andy asked.

"I'm not entirely sure yet," she said, lifting her gaze to his dark eyes. Andy frowned and Quinn looked away.

"Quinn," Andy said gently. "You can't go off by yourself."

Quinn shifted back into her chair, looking tired.

"There's something I need to find out," she said.

Andy inhaled. "Your theory?" he asked.

So she'd told him the world wasn't real, too. Seemed she must tell that to most people she met.

"It's not a theory," Quinn said. "It's the truth. I don't know why no one else knows. But I do. And I have to find out why."

Andy looked at her empathetically, but not with pity.

Allie blurted out, "I'm inclined to believe you, darlin', but I ain't got much influence in convincing the rest of the world." She paused. "What was it again?"

Andy downed the rest of his tea, and took Wade and Quinn's empty cups.

"Alright, Ma. Time to head back up," he said, helping her out of her chair.

"Alright then," she said.

someone

She pulled Quinn into her arms.

"Goodbye, Quinnie," Allie said. "I'll see you soon!"

"Goodbye, Ma," Quinn replied. "Thank you."

"And I hope to see you soon, as well. Mister Walker," Allie said to Wade. She winked at him.

Wade just nodded. Andy and Missy got her back up the stairs. Andy returned a moment later and took Quinn aside. Wade stood by, pretending he couldn't hear them.

"I wish you wouldn't do this," Andy said. "You scared the living daylights out of us, Quinn."

She crossed her arms, closed off to him.

"I know," she said. "I'm sorry. For so long I've been told that there's something wrong with me. I can't take it anymore."

Andy offered a small smile.

"I never said that," he said. "You're the smartest person I know. You may be a little strange sometimes..."

He ruffled her hair in a brotherly way. She glared at him admonishingly.

"And something really odd happened to me the other day..." Quinn went on after a few moments. "Something that might help me prove what I've been saying."

He looked thoughtful for a moment.

"Okay," he said. "But...I'll come with you. You need-"

"No," Quinn interrupted firmly. "I'll be fine. Look..."

She pulled Catherine's revolver from its holster.

Andy shook his head. "I thought it got tossed in the pond?" he said.

"Found a new one," she said, with a guilty sideways glance.

"Uh-huh," Andy said. "But I'm still going."

Quinn, exasperated, said, "No. You've got Ma and Missy to take care of, and you're the sheriff now."

"I'm going," Wade said.

Quinn glanced at him. "What?" she said.

"I'll go with you," Wade said.

"Why?" Quinn asked.

"I accepted responsibility for you after what happened in Birch," he said. "Seems I ought to make sure you don't go getting into trouble again."

Quinn frowned. "Fine," she said.

She turned to Andy. "Goodbye, Andy."

"Goodbye, Quinn," Andy said, solemnly.

She took his hand and squeezed it. "I'll come back. I'll find you."

Andy nodded. "You better."

He let them out and closed the door behind them, not before Wade saw the pained look on his face.

Quinn led the way back outside of town, toward the hill she'd been heading for earlier.

"Why don't you stay with them?" Wade asked. "They seem like good people."

"They are," she said. She paused, looking up at Wade with determination in her eyes. "But I can't stay. Something's just wrong. Either with me or everyone else. And if I don't figure it out, I reckon I really will lose my mind."

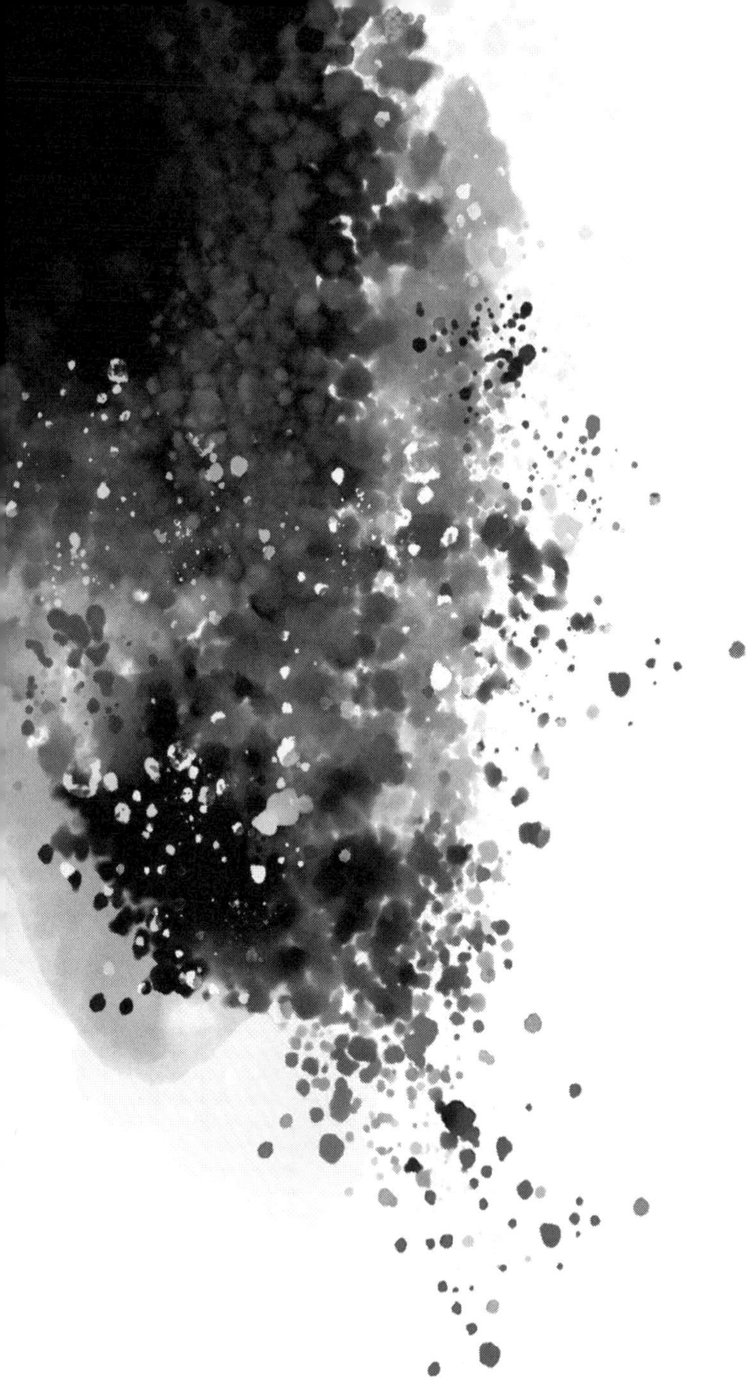

someone

IV

Andy had been Quinn's friend since she was eight, and he was twelve. Allie was donating his old clothes to the orphanage. It had been the dead of winter. Quinn was sitting outside, no coat, freezing for the sake of being rebellious.

Three times she had been irately told to come in, and three times she had irately refused. Anything to cause trouble for them. She would be three times beaten when she did finally go inside, though not as badly as when she'd told them the world was not real.

So there she'd been, sitting outside freezing, when he brought her one of his old coats.

"Why are you out here?" he had asked.

"I hate it inside," she answered.

"Oh," he said. "Me too."

And so they became best friends. They played together, and she'd had dinner with him and his grandmother often.

She'd helped him work up the courage to marry Missy two years ago. He didn't say she was crazy- though he did not believe her, she knew. The Connors made life in Oak bearable. They were the reason she had not run away long ago.

When she left a few days ago, she said nothing. If she had told them she was leaving, Andy would've stopped her, or tried to go with her, as he had today. She couldn't let him do that. His ma, whose mind was slowly slipping, and delicate, sweet-natured Missy, needed him.

The sun had reached the one o'clock position, and sweat crept along the back of her neck, wetting her red bandana.

"Where'd you get your revolver?" she asked Wade, trying to take her mind off the heat.

"Town I used to live at, called Hickory," he said coolly.

"What was your job?" she said.

He grumbled a bit to himself before answering. "I was

the sheriff," he said.

"Ha!" Quinn exclaimed. "I knew it. Why'd you leave?"

"I got voted out," Wade said. "People claiming I was trigger-happy, abusing my power..."

"Were you?" she asked.

He glanced over at her, surprised by the question.

"No," he said simply. "Folks tend to forget that you're the only thing standing between peace and all hell breaking loose with that job. Sometimes it takes a little more than kind words of reprimand when you're dealing with murderers, rapists, and thieves. But people will yet call for the release of Barabbas."

Quinn stood silently for a moment, thinking over his words.

"I reckon you were a good lawman," she said.

Andy was a good one too, though he could probably learn a thing or two from Wade. Andy was persuasive but reluctant to hurt anyone. He had pulled his gun a few times during his year on the job, but never had to shoot. She feared that someday his words would not be able to save him.

"I don't know about that," Wade said. "But I sure tried to be. Didn't end up getting me anywhere, though."

"Got you here," Quinn said.

"Sure enough," Wade mumbled.

Half an hour later, they were approaching the hill.

"People always told the kids this hill was haunted," Quinn said. "Nobody ever came up here. I did…" She counted on her fingers. "Four days ago. To get my bearings. Then my memory blanks-"

"What do you mean, it blanks?" Wade interrupted.

"I don't know!" Quinn said forcefully. "It just does. The next thing I remember is being in the street in Birch, and running into you."

"Huh," Wade said.

Quinn sighed.

"Let me tell you everything I know," she said. "Don't interrupt, just listen. Please?"

Wade nodded.

"This world isn't real. I have always known that. I don't know how…or what it is. The real world…"

That sharp pain in her head from a few days ago returned. She squinted.

"The real world is...it's called..."

She covered her eyes with her palms. She was trying to say the word *Terra*. The pain expanded into her neck and shoulders. She found herself on her knees.

"Missy Quinn?" Wade was saying. "What's wrong with you?"

She had to get that blasted word out.

The real world is called Terra... Terra...Why can't I say it?

This had never happened. Not before Wednesday. But before Wednesday, she realized, she had never known the word Terra. There was a memory there. Something that was trying to rise to the surface.

Come on!

"The...real...world..." she ground out. "It's called... called... Terra! It's called *Terra*!"

She blacked out.

When Quinn came to, her head ached worse than it ever had before. The first thing she saw was the night sky. The stars seemed too bright, and hurt her eyes.

She looked around, smelling smoke. Wade had a fire going nearby.

"The real world is called...*that word* you said," he said. "I heard it, but I can't say it, nor think it, nor recall it."

Quinn sat up.

"It's driving me crazy," he continued. "I should remember it, but I just can't. Can you tell me again? Or will you black out again? Dangit, girl, I thought you had dropped dead."

Quinn stuck a finger in the dirt beside her, trying something different. Maybe she could write it down. She'd barely gotten past the first two letters when pain zinged through her skull. It took a few moments for her to be able to speak.

"I'll black out again, I reckon," she said. "I wish I could. I can think it, I just can't say it without..."

"Huh," said Wade. "Well, it's strange...Isn't sitting well with me. How's your head now?"

"Still aching," Quinn said. "But I think it's getting better." She paused. "What do you remember from your childhood?"

someone

He thought a moment.

"I...I suppose I don't remember anything," he finally said. "Why?"

"My first memory is twelve years ago," she said. "Arriving at the orphanage."

Wade's brows drew together, contemplatively.

"What is it?" she asked.

"I do remember twelve years ago," he said. "When I got to Hickory. I was... thirty-six. But..."

He twisted a metal band around and around on his finger, brows furrowed. His eyes fell on the thin, dull piece of metal, and he examined it for a moment. When he looked up at her again, his face was clouded with confusion.

"I don't remember anything before that." He took off his hat, ran a hand through his hair. "What is going on here?"

"That's what I aim to find out," she said, laying back down. "But in the morning..."

Sunday dawned a few hours later. Quinn's head had ceased its aching, and she opened her eyes to see Wade sitting up, flipping through a small book. She watched silently as he read, newborn light accentuating the look of rumination on his face. He closed the book and his eyes, chin dipping toward his chest and hat obscuring his face.

The fire had mostly died, and Quinn stood and stomped out the remaining embers. She scuffed dirt over it with her boot, then opened up her pack. She pulled out the jerky she had taken from Catherine.

"Head still hurting?" Wade asked, looking up.

Quinn shook her head, tossing him a piece of jerky.

"Let's go," she said.

Wade stood and they started the trek up the hill.

"What exactly are you looking to find up here?" he said.

"I'm not entirely sure," Quinn said. "I'll figure out the last spot I remember, and we'll see."

She looked around. There. She remembered that bush. The red shirt she had been wearing had caught on it. The hill was somewhat rocky. She remembered sliding a little bit. Wade raised his brows and indicated that they keep going. Then she began to hear something: a low humming noise.

Wawawawa...

They kept going.

Wawawawawawa...

A feeling of static encompassed her whole body. All of her hair stood on end, from the hair on her head to the hair on her legs.

Wade's hair was concealed underneath his hat, but the fuzz on his arms stood up. He looked at her in both utter amazement and bewilderment.

A memory struck her. This happened the first time she was here. The static electricity, the humming. She looked around. Perhaps this hill was haunted. What else could cause...this? But Quinn did not believe in ghosts.

She kept moving. It was terrifying, but familiar. She had done this before. The world around her was collapsing into itself, folding in and out, breaking apart and coming back together. Waxing and waning. Pulsating and immobile. She looked back. Wade was making his way toward her.

Up ahead she saw something odd- a faint shimmer, or light, or reflection. She walked toward it. The searing pain in her head returned with a vengeance. She kept walking. Her legs felt heavy.

Come on...come on...

There was the shimmer again, very close up ahead. Waves of hot pain zinged into her skull. Her chest hurt. She drew near the light. Almost there...She reached out with her left hand and found an erratic reflection of herself. The elongated fingers of her reflection touched the tips of her real ones, then her real fingers passed through the reflection. Then went her hand, her forearm, her shoulder, the left side of her body, and finally the right side.

It was terribly cold and all was black for an instant of mortifying uncertainty. Then she found herself lying on a smooth, cool floor, shivering. She did not yet open her eyes, but felt around her body, making sure all was intact.

Finally, she opened her eyes. She sat in a dim, empty room. She stood, turned around, and could clearly see what she had just left. There was Wade, wandering through the static electricity. He was calling out, probably for her. She turned and looked around the rest of the room. It was unlike any room she could remember seeing before, but somehow familiar.

She concentrated hard. Where was she? Why was it familiar? Had she gotten out...out of...*there*? Was she now in...Terra? She opened her mouth and whispered it.

"Terra."

No pain, no blackout, no repercussions. She said it again.

"Terra."

A memory wafted into her mind. She had stumbled through the static electricity, and through that...wall. She had been in this room, wearing her red shirt, trousers, and split skirt. Beyond that, she remembered nothing.

She cautiously walked the room. There was no furniture, no windows. But she found a door. It was the same color as the walls and ceiling, and difficult to tell apart from the rest of the room. But she was almost positive it was a door. She returned to the wall and looked out at Wade.

"Wade!" she started to shout, then thought better of it.

Come on. You're almost there! We found something.

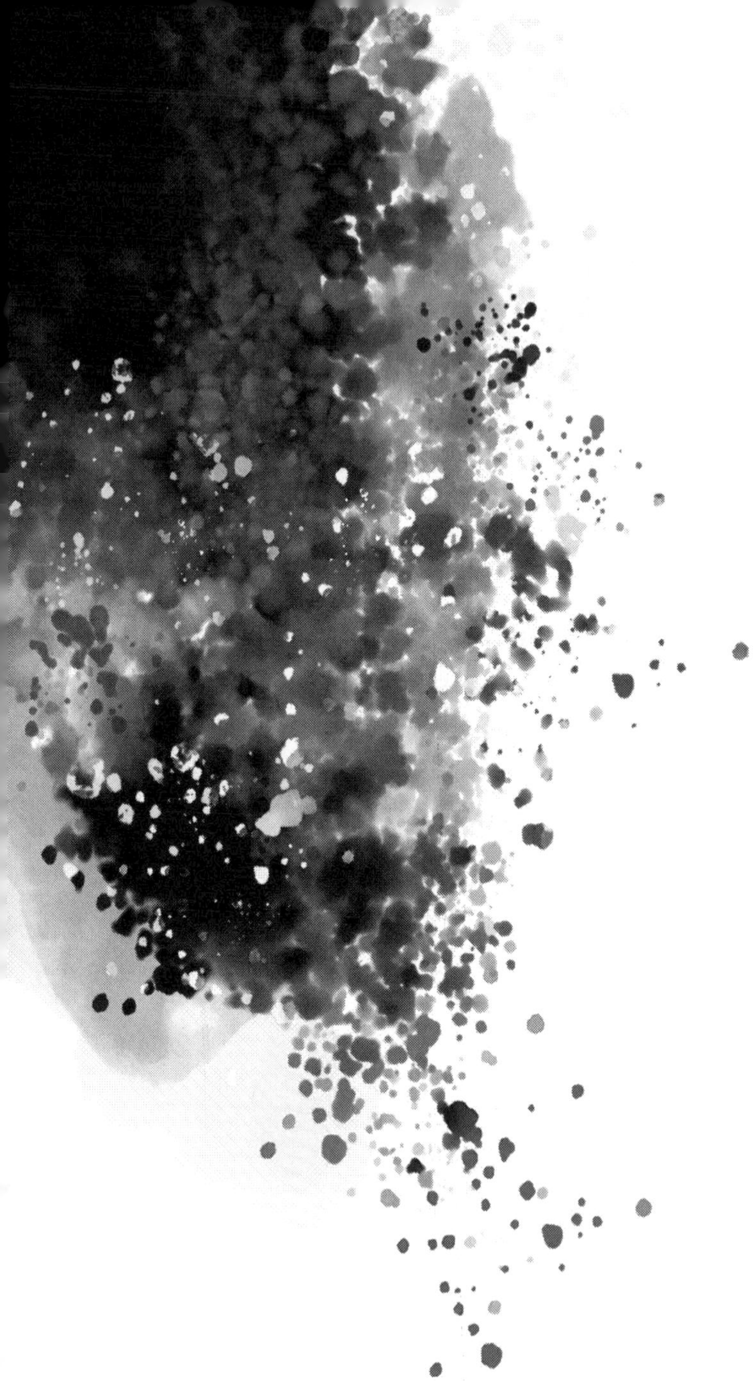

someone

V

Where did she go?

The girl had disappeared into thin air. Wade trudged forward, looking for a sign of Quinn. Good Lord, what was he doing here? He had lost his own mind, surely, following that crazy girl into something all kinds of wrong. He saw a glimmer up ahead.

"Quinn!" he hollered. "Quinn!"

Where could she have gone? Was there a cliff ahead that she could have fallen from? He kept going, watching his feet. The **wawawawawa** noise thrummed in his ears. A sharp pain pierced through his head. He saw the glimmer again. His legs grew heavier, then he found himself staring at an elongated picture of himself. Past that...there was Quinn. He could barely see her, waving, trying to get his attention.

He reached out and his reflected hand met his real one. His hand disappeared! His arm disappeared! Everything disappeared. It was freezing and black...and then he was lying on a cool smooth surface.

Wade opened his eyes. There stood Quinn.

"You made it," she said with a sigh.

Wade looked around. Behind him, through a sort of portal, he could see what he had just left. Around them, a bare room, with no windows. It was dim, and he could not see a door anywhere.

"Where are we?" he asked.

Quinn looked around.

"I'm not sure...but I can say the word now," she said in an excited hurry. "It's Terra. The real world is Terra."

He remembered it, he thought it, then he said it, "Terra."

It seemed familiar to him, in a disconcerting sort of way.

"I've been here before," Quinn said. "On Monday. It just

came back to me. I made it through the static and into this room...but then it blanks."

Wade scratched his head. "No door in here," he acknowledged.

"There is," Quinn said, motioning for him to follow her.

He stood and walked to the other side of the room with her.

"I didn't see it at first, either," she said. "It blends with the rest of the room. But it looks like a door, doesn't it?"

He nodded. "Did you try to open it?"

"Not yet."

She pushed against it. Nothing happened. Wade felt around the door's cracks. He could feel cool air coming through. Choosing to ignore and not attempt to explain what he had just experienced, he set about trying to get the thing opened. He worked his fingers into a groove that ran along the length of it and pulled. Nothing.

He motioned Quinn over and both of them pulled, to no avail. They stepped back, out of breath. Quinn walked around the room again, investigating.

"There's nothing else here, at least that I can tell," she

said.

Wade glanced back at the wall leading outside. He crossed the room and reached out to touch it. It felt cold and solid- they could not go back through. He didn't like that. He returned to Quinn, who leaned back on the wall beside the door. Abruptly, the door slid open, so fast he barely saw it move. Quinn jumped.

"What!" she exclaimed. She investigated the area she had just leaned on. "There's a little raised circle here."

She poked it with her pointer finger. The door slid closed again.

"What sort of witchcraft is that?" Wade asked.

"I don't know," Quinn said. "I've never seen anything like it."

She opened the door again. They walked out cautiously. A hall spread to their left and right. There was a series of windows on the far side of it. It was substantially brighter than the room. Quinn, after glancing both ways, went to the window.

"Whoa," she breathed. "Come here."

Wade walked across to her.

someone

"What?" he said, then saw. "Oh."

There lay a strange landscape, unlike anything he had ever seen before. The sky was black -though it was daytime- and the ground was a pale, dusty white. There was a complex of odd, metal constructions sprinkled about the strange landscape. And far away, past the horizon's end, Wade saw a large, glowing...moon? But much larger, and blue and green and obscured by grayish swirls...

"What on earth?" Quinn said.

Wade did not like this.

Then he saw a strange creature. It had the bodily proportions of a man, but its head was huge and black, with no features. Its body was covered in white folds and tubes. It bounded across the surface, weightless. How was that possible? Where were they? Wade was beginning to doubt his consciousness, his sanity...but Quinn was walking away, down the left hallway. He took off after her.

"Where are you going?" he asked.

"To find...something!" she said. "Something that can explain this. Where are we?"

"You think I know?" he said irately.

He had not expected this. It was so...otherworldly. Yet somehow it evoked familiarity. That almost scared him more than the blasted place itself. He could not stop looking out those windows. That black sky was terrifying. Why was the sky black?

There was a left turn up ahead. Quinn paused at the corner, peeked around it, and then continued. Wade followed, growing more and more uneasy. There was something on the edge of his mind. A memory, he thought, trying to surface, but not quite able to. Quinn stopped.

"Look," she said, pointing to the wall.

It was a door, like the one they had left. There was a raised circle alongside it. Beside it was another door, and another. On and on. The opposite wall was the same.

Finally they reached the end of the hallway. There was a door there, and Quinn opened it. It led to a small chamber, with some sort of hatch on the opposite side. There were large beige backpacks sitting on the floor, and three white lumps of material hanging on the wall. They were like absurdly thick long johns, and there were three black dome-shaped helmets sitting nearby. That's what the creature outside had been wearing! So it wasn't a creature. Just a man wearing that strange clothing. There was a sign above the clothes that read, "Do not open door unless chamber is sealed and suits are on properly."

Just then, the hatch opened. The air rushed out, and Wade grabbed hold of Quinn with one hand and grasped the table where the helmets sat with the other. He attempted to breathe but could get no oxygen. The creature -or, man in a suit- walked through the door. He jumped at the sight of them, and shut the door behind him.

Air quickly refilled the room and Wade inhaled. The man in the suit removed his helmet and stared at them for a moment. He had light brown skin and long, wavy hair.

"What..." he began, then pulled a device from somewhere on his person. "Help! I am in the oxygen chamber at the northern exit. Subjects have breached-"

Wade whacked him across the head with one of the huge round helmets.

"Come on," Wade said, turning and opening the door.

They ran back into the hallway.

"Wait!" Quinn said, and dashed into the room.

She grabbed two of the white suits and a bag, and they started running, back the way they'd come. Wade heard footsteps. He grabbed hold of Quinn, opened one of the doors to a portal-room, and shoved her in. The room was identical to the one they'd come from, except its portal showed a different scene. He recognized it as being outside his old town, Hickory.

Wade grumbled to himself, dragging his hand down his face. Quinn was trying to figure out the suits. She found the opening and managed to pull one of them on. It was huge, and the crotch of the pants hung at her knees. She rolled the legs at the ankles and tossed the other suit to Wade.

"How do you..." he began, but she had already opened it.

He shrugged off his old backpack and held out the suit. He stepped into the legs and closed it up. It fit him about right, he supposed. He wasn't sure how it was supposed to fit. Quinn was pulling items out of her bag and transferring them to the large one she'd found.

"This bag blends better," she said, tucking a box of bullets and a canteen into the pack.

He nodded, opening up his own bag. There wasn't much inside- some jerky, several boxes of extra ammunition, his hunting knife, a spare shirt. He kept most necessities on his person, in his pockets.

Wade contributed the jerky, ammo, and knife to the bag.

"Do you really need that knife?" Quinn asked.

"Do you really need an answer to that question?" he returned.

"Fair enough."

He took off his hat and shoved it inside, and Quinn did the same. He closed the backpack, slid his arms into the straps. They tossed their own bags into a corner and left the room.

A group of men and women wearing grey suits were running down the hallway, holding odd guns. They ran right past, barely noticing Wade and Quinn.

When they came to the fork in the hall, they turned back where they'd first come out. They passed the first room, and kept running that way.

"Hey!" someone shouted.

Wade turned. There was a man behind them, wearing a

white suit.

"Are you John and Kinsey?" the man said. "Unit Four?"

Wade stuttered. What was the most unsuspicious answer to that question?

"Uh, yeah," he finally said.

"Come on," said the man. "Your unit is leaving without you." He stared at Quinn. "Make sure you get a different suit. That one has a very ill fit."

She nodded. The man lowered his brows, giving them a curious look, then started down the hallway.

"Kinsey?" said Quinn. "What kind of name is Kinsey?"

"What kind of name is Quinn?" Wade said.

She rolled her eyes. Another voice boomed through the hallway.

"Unit Four! All Unit Four personnel, report to the launch chamber."

"I guess that's us," Wade said.

He spotted double doors up ahead. A sign above them read Launch Chamber.

"There!" he said.

They ran to the doors and he yanked one open. They

stumbled in to find a line of men and women, all wearing the same white suits. They were entering a huge, cone-shaped...what was it? A vehicle? A building? Whatever it was, they were entering it.

Wade and Quinn rushed to the back of the line. And then they stood there, for a long, long while.

It was taking an absurd amount of time for everyone to enter the long cone-shaped whatever it was. Wade judged that twenty minutes passed before they finally reached the front. When they did, a man in a grey suit escorted them inside.

They were brought into a long, narrow room with two opposite-facing rows of chairs, each of them fitted with various straps and some odd mechanism on the back. Most of the seats were already filled. All who were seated had their eyes closed. Were they asleep?

The man took Wade and Quinn to their seats, and stashed the big bag in a nearby compartment. Her seat was behind his. He watched as the man secured Quinn's straps. They went over her chest, her lap, and bound her wrists to the armrests. A heavy looking helmet was lowered over her head and neck, so that she could not move them. Wade could see panic on her face. A whir sounded, and a metallic arm, with a needle on the end, appeared from somewhere on the chair.

"What is that?" Quinn demanded, petrified as it moved above the crook of her elbow. "What is that? Hey, wai-"

The needle shot into her arm, and her eyes rolled back into her head before their lids fell shut. The man walked over to Wade, and he sat down in his own chair.

"I would have thought she had never done this before," the man remarked as he began strapping him in.

Wade tried to smile, or something, but he couldn't. The straps were digging into his chest, thighs, and wrists, and *oh man*, he couldn't turn his head. He tried to maintain a placid expression. Then he heard the whir. He couldn't look but knew that needle was coming. He jerked against the restraints.

"What, you too?" said the man. "Be still."

Wade felt the prick in his arm, and then nothing at all.

someone

VI

Swish.

The rocket's hatch slides open. The six-year-old girl is whisked inside by a woman with black hair. She is led to a seat and made to sit down.

Snap.

Her restraints are in place. Her eyes fly up to the woman strapping her into the seat.

"Where am I going?"

The woman pauses, then tells her. She won't remember anyway.

"To the moon," the woman says. "For Terra's new project, Operation Retrospect. Studying the past by recreating

it. It will be a whole new world."

"Like this one?" the girl asks.

"No," the woman snaps. "The world you are going to is not real. It is an experiment, placing people in simulations of past time periods to study said time periods."

The girl does not know what the woman is talking about. She hears sobbing from somewhere else in the rocket. Her eyes flick all around as she tries to see what is happening, unable to turn her head. On the opposite row, she spots a man with wavy hair. His light brown eyes are sad, but he smiles at her.

Prick.

Quinn jumped into wakefulness. It was dark, and she was still pinned down by the straps. But she could remember. She remembered boarding a rocket, just like this one, and arriving on the moon. Being put to sleep there, and then arriving at the orphanage in Oak.

Wade had been there. On the very same rocket as her.

She did not remember anything before that. Or what the real world was like. Nor could she yet remember what had happened a few days ago, when she first passed through the portal. But it was coming! Her memories were coming back.

"Wade," she whispered. "Wade?"

She heard a cough.

"Quinn?" Wade whispered, sounding groggy.

"Here I am," she responded.

"I...remembered something," Wade said. "Or, someone. I remembered being on a...rocket, like this one. I saw a little girl there. She looked kinda like you."

"I think it was me," she said. "I remember you, too."

"But that was all," he continued. "Why were we there?"

"I remember a woman telling me," Quinn said. "She said it was Terra's new project, Operation...Remember? No, Retrospect. Operation Retrospect. She said that they were studying the past by recreating it, with simulations. On the moon."

"What?" Wade said loudly. "The moon?"

Another voice, a man's, spoke up from the darkness, "Who is that?"

"Er, John," Wade said. "Sorry."

The voice mumbled something that Quinn could not understand. She and Wade said no more. Presently, she heard the sounds of others waking. Then a bright light snapped on. She squinted. She could see the back of Wade's chair in front of her. A man, not the one from before, came from a door at the front of the room and began loosing people from their restraints.

"Hello," he said to a woman he was releasing. "Welcome back. How are things going up there?"

"Fairly well," she replied. "It sounded like two subjects had somehow managed to make it through a sim-gate, but I am sure they will be apprehended. There is nowhere for them to go."

He went down the row, making small talk and releasing each person. Quinn was the eighth person on their row, so it took several minutes for him to reach her.

"I have not seen you before," he said as he unfastened the strap over her legs.

"This was my first time…there," she said.

"Ah. Exciting?" he asked.

"Very," Quinn said.

She nodded in thanks as he moved on to Wade's seat.

After he was released, they got their bag from the compartment. Thankfully, the people running this operation didn't seem to bother with checking anyone's belongings.

They exited the ship. Quinn blinked in the sunlight and took a breath. It was fresher than the air she had been breathing for twelve years, and colder. The air on...the moon... had been stale.

She inclined her head and gazed at the sky. It had so much more depth to it. It was *real*. She looked around, taking it all in. They were surrounded by a high fence, and outside snow covered the ground. Her breath crystallized in the air and her face tingled. It was refreshing.

Wade grasped her arm. The group was moving along. Ahead, she could see an odd building. It was painted white, sleek, and nothing like the structures she was used to seeing. She supposed that the buildings back...on the moon... were what things used to look like. This was what they looked like now.

There was a sort of tower beside the white building, and at the top she could see a man holding an odd black gun. Wade caught her attention and nodded his head toward a line forming at the entrance of the small building.

"They're giving a card to the person there," he said. "We don't have cards."

Quinn dipped her chin.

"We have to get out of here," she said. "Over the fence, or something."

"He'll see us," Wade said, lifting his eyes to the tower.

"Hmm," Quinn said. She glanced around. "Look. The right side of that building is out of his line of sight. Just have to get over there, and climb that fence without being seen."

"Hey!" someone shouted; he looked like a guard. "Get in line!"

They hurried to get in the line. Quinn got an idea. She clamped her hand over her mouth and began heaving. Wade, catching on, grabbed her and hauled her over to the side of the building, where she continued fake vomiting.

"Are you alright?" asked a man brave enough to investigate.

"She's fine," Wade said. "Just feeling sort of sick, after, you know, the journey."

someone

Apparently the man was deterred and disappeared.

"Go on. Hurry up."

She scaled the fence, then perched atop it while Wade climbed up. The fence was a little lower than the roof of the white building, keeping them from the view of the watch tower.

"Now where?" Quinn asked.

"Mm-mm," Wade said.

"Great," Quinn said. "Very informative."

Wade dropped to the ground, and Quinn followed suit.

"This way," he said, moving toward the back of the building. They ducked under the windows as they went.

"Stupid...snow," Wade muttered, looking back over the tracks they had left.

Anyone would easily be able to find them following that trail. When they reached the corner of the building, Wade peeked around the edge.

"There's no window on the back of the tower," he said. "The sniper won't see us go that way."

He pointed to their right, into the white wilderness. They started running. Snow crunched under Quinn's boots, making a pleasing sound.

This seemed to be a mountainous area. There were few trees, and the ones that did inhabit the place were dry and leafless. Quinn looked back over her shoulder to see if they were being followed.

She noticed too late that Wade had pulled up short. Her stomach dropped as she went over the edge of a cliff steeper than anyone could survive a fall from. A hand grabbed the back of her suit, holding her dangling over the cliff for a moment before pulling her back to the ground. She landed on her bottom, hard.

"Watch where you're going," Wade said.

She nodded.

"Hey," she said. "Look. There's a ledge right there. Make your footprints end here too. We can walk along that edge. Maybe they'll think we fell off."

He shrugged.

"Worth a shot, I guess," he said.

They carefully climbed down to the small ledge. Both of their footprints stopped at the cliff. It could be assumed that they had plummeted to their deaths. There was no snow on the ledge, though it was icy. Quinn made sure she kept one hand on the rock at all times.

"You remember anything else?" Wade asked.

"No," Quinn said.

"I do," Wade said. "I remember being eighteen years old. I was in...a doctor's office. They were testing me."

"For what?" Quinn asked.

"For who I would marry," he said. "To find someone I would be compatible with. They do that to everyone! All the eighteen-year-olds. It's one of...Terra's laws."

"Why?" Quinn inquired.

"I don't...I don't remember," he said.

She could tell he was thinking hard. "So were you paired?" she said.

He remained quiet for a few moments. "No," he said. "I wasn't."

"Why not?"

"I don't remember yet."

He went silent. Obviously there was science and technology in the real world she knew nothing of. Wade remembered because he had lived much longer in Terra.

Quinn realized that she would probably never remember her short prior life. How did they choose who they sent? Why her? Why Wade? Why Andy and Allie?

As they walked along the edge, she recapped for herself. They'd come through what the woman on the rocket called a sim-gate, into the base of whoever organized the whole thing; the Terrian government? The base was on the moon. She was still having trouble with that one. The moon she had looked upon at night was a false one, and the earth she had walked upon was, too. How was Wade handling that?

"Wade?" she said.

"Yes, Missy Quinn?" he replied.

Tension had crept into his voice since they passed through the static field, and it remained there.

"How're you holding up?" she asked.

It took about two minutes for him to answer. And it was only a disconcerted and somewhat ireful sigh. She bit her lip. She had yet to understand his accompanying her. She was increasingly grateful that he was.

"Wade?" she said.

"Hmm?" he mumbled.

"Why're you here?" she asked.

"I don't know," he said. "I just thought someone should accompany you to your destination. And then…things stopped lining up. Your nonsense started to make sense. May as well try to stay alive long enough to understand it."

She heard people above and behind them.

"Where did they go?" a male voice asked.

"Look," said another. "The prints end at the cliff."

A third voice, this one female, asked, "Did they fall off?"

Quinn and Wade remained perfectly motionless. She held her breath. The three people murmured quietly. She could not understand what they were saying for a few moments.

"I think that they fell off the cliff," said the first man.

Quiet agreements came from the other two. Footsteps crunched away, back toward the small building. A few minutes later, they resumed inching their way along the edge.

After what Quinn judged to be an hour, they came to the end of the ledge. Wade stopped and looked over his shoulder.

"Look," said Wade. "It'll be a big jump, but there's a

spot down there..."

He pointed to a small shelf of rock three feet down from the end of the ledge. A small, sad-looking tree sprouted from it, and it looked quite icy.

"Come here," Wade said.

She moved up next to him, and he whisked her to the other side of him. Quinn prepared to jump.

"Watch out for that ice," he said.

She bent her legs and stepped off the edge; it was more a calculated fall than a jump, requiring a little push to make the distance. She landed, slipped, and fell on her rear, bruising her hip in the process.

"You alright?" Wade asked from above.

"Yeah," she answered, scooting back to make room for him to land.

She grasped a protrusion of rock. He stepped off the edge, landing with his knees bent and avoiding a slip.

"Now where?" Quinn asked.

Wade looked around, pursing his lips. He got on his knees, peering over the edge.

"Eh," he said. "We just stay here for now."

She nodded and rubbed her bruised hip. That was going to be right sore tomorrow. She leaned against the rockface, and Wade sat next to her.

Quinn closed her eyes, thinking back to that Monday when she had first climbed Oak Hill. She concentrated hard. In her mind's eye, she pictured herself in the clothing she had been wearing: her red shirt, split skirt, trousers, and boots. She recalled climbing the hill, and her shirt getting caught in the bush. She remembered being in the field of static electricity, and passing through the sim-gate, and the sheer terror of finding herself in that room. She had been trapped in there for hours, she remembered.

Then, someone had entered the room. He was wearing a grey suit and jumped when he saw her. She remembered reaching for her revolver, which was not there- Ava Mark had taken it away. The man had called in more people, and they had dragged her out, down the hallway, into a room with a small metal table and many strange instruments.

They had poked and prodded her all over. They had stuffed her into that long white shirt and strapped her to the table. She had thrashed and thrashed, even scored a kick to one man's face, but could not escape. A man wearing a white coat had entered. He placed something sticky on her temples. She heard a negative-sounding beep.

"Her memory-block microchip has a malfunction," he'd said. "I am not sure how much she knows, but it cannot stay that way. Knock her out so that I can fix it."

"What should we do when you are through?"

"Try putting her in another town. Let us see how they react to that."

Someone shoved a needle into her wrist, and she had felt herself draining away. But not before she felt the knife on her head. She reached up and felt the spot where she remembered the cut. It took a few moments, but she found it under her hair, near the center on the side of her head. A fresh scar. She shuddered at the hazy recollection, the fear fresh in her mind again.

"Wade?" she said.

His hand went to his forehead, as if the very sound of her voice caused him pain.

"Yeah?" he said, tired.

She told him all that she had remembered. He did not

someone

respond for several minutes.

"Memory-blocking microchips," Wade finally said. "I don't quite know what that is, but I can speculate as to what it means."

He paused, formulating his hypothesis thoroughly.

"They put some sort of machinery in everyone up there's heads that makes them forget the real world. And yours doesn't work, even after they tried to fix it."

"I suppose it stops working completely when you pass through that...sim-gate, they called it," Quinn said.

Wade nodded.

"Well," he said. "I don't remember everything about this real world yet. But the thing I do know is that something here is very wrong."

It hadn't taken him long to think over those words.

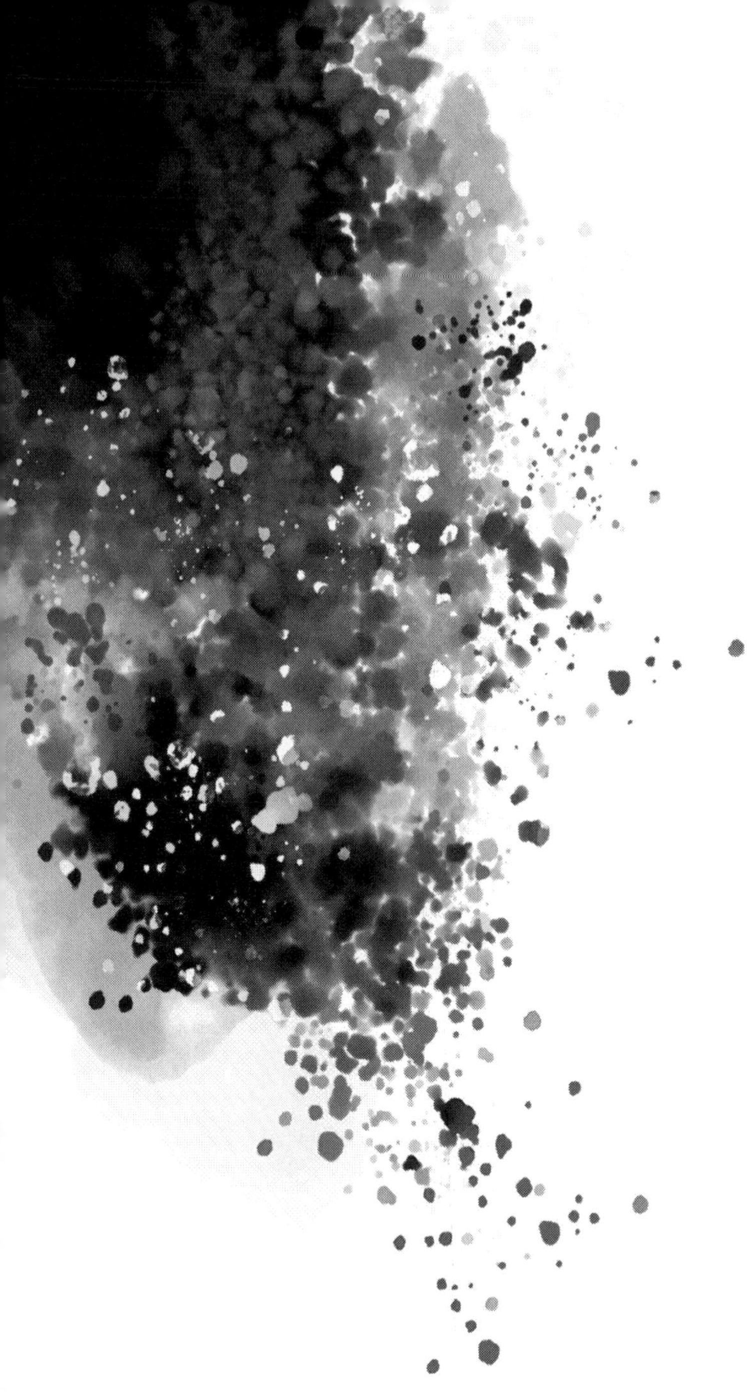

VII

Wade sat awake thinking, long after Quinn fell asleep. More and more random memories drifted into his head. Growing up in a large City. Swimming in a heavily chlorinated pool as a child. Watching a small box with a screen called a television. He had no recollection of his parents, and supposed that he had none.

He recalled what seemed to be voting when he was a young adult, though he did not remember what it was for. He remembered the pair testing he underwent at age eighteen. He was denied his pairing and sent to an RT, one of the compounds where people useless to Terra went...

And then came everything else.

Oh, God...

Wade pushed the heels of his hands into his eyes as his mind filled with long-hidden memories. A wave of repressed emotions rolled in. Guilt and grief and hatred, twelve years dormant, lambasted him all at once. Pressure welled in his chest, his eyes and throat burned.

Oh, God.

What they had done to him.

With his memories was coming an understanding of this world. The government controlled everything. Population, education, media, economics. Everything.

Wade also recalled how different he'd been. Before Operation Retrospect, he'd been a different person. Angry, spiteful, venomous. He'd even spoken differently. He had used no contractions, had no accent. He had not known of such things as guns or Jesus. Or even the grasp of right and wrong that he now had.

One could make the point that they had all been created as part of the illusion, but it was supposed to be a reconstruction of reality, of history. So he reckoned that those were real things, but Terra had somehow done away with the knowledge of them. They were from before.

But what was before? As hard as he tried to remember, he found nothing regarding history. Save for the fact that apparently the last twelve years of his life were a simulation of some part of it. He rubbed his temples, sad and tired and angry.

Seeing those memories in his mind's eye was like watching someone else live them. Except it was him. He had lived those things, had done those things. He had known more and less. As difficult as it was to wrap his mind around the whole enormous ridiculous truth, it was that: the truth.

As bad as it hurt him, he was glad that he knew. Because that meant he could do something about it.

A word he had learned sometime in the last twelve years drifted into his mind, one he had not known prior to being a part of Operation Retrospect. That word was *revolution*.

At some point, he drifted off to sleep. In the morning he woke to Quinn gnawing on jerky. She had removed her spacesuit -as he now knew it to be called- and returned her little hat to her head. The bag sat beside her, opened. She handed him some beef jerky and her canteen.

"Mornin'," she said.

He nodded in return. He decided that climbing would be easier -though it would be colder- if he removed his spacesuit, so he did. He scanned their surroundings. To their left, he could see a way down the rockface. It would not be easy, and they were still high up.

"What's on your mind?" she asked.

He raised his brows. "Hmm?" he mumbled.

Quinn repeated her question.

"My memories came back," he said.

"All of them?" she said.

"Uh-huh," he said. "Near about. It seems I was what they deemed a criminal." He smirked, but the expression didn't reach his eyes. "Kinda funny, seeing how they made me the lawman in the...experiment."

Quinn set her chin in her hand. "What was it like?" she asked.

He thought for a moment, trying to get it all straight before he spoke.

"I had no parents, and I was raised with a group of other children in a City. Everyone who complies and produces well lives in the Cities. At the age of eighteen I was tested for a spouse, and did not receive one due to my genetic impurity. Then they shipped me off to what they call an RT- a compound, er, a town, where people rejected from the matching policy go. I lived there a long time."

He paused, studying the metal encircling his fourth finger.

"I got into trouble, and made the deal that if I became a part of their Operation Retrospect, it would be alright. And then, you know, the moon and all that."

He folded his hands, looked away and breathed. Quinn sat silently for a moment.

"I'm sorry," she finally said. "I suppose you'd rather have not known."

"No," Wade replied. "Knowing means I can do something about it."

Quinn nodded, her brows drawn together in thought.

"And I now have an advantage," he continued.

"What's that?" she asked.

"I'm the only man in this forsaken place that knows how

to shoot a real gun," he said.

"I can shoot," Quinn stated.

"Eh, sure," Wade said. "Some of their men have things a little like guns." He tapped his holster. "But not real ones like ours."

He grabbed the pack and slipped his arms into the straps.

"You and I, girl, are about to give old Terra a sucker punch," he said.

"What do you mean?" Quinn asked.

"I mean," Wade said. "You and I are fixing to start a revolution."

VIII

Revolution? Quinn thought.

Wade had a different sort of look on his face, one she had not yet seen. There was a certain ardor in his eyes that had not been there before. His face was transformed. He looked younger, bolder, no longer passive. Yet there was also an acute hurt in his eyes which she hadn't seen until now; something much more there that he wasn't telling.

Wade had been wronged and was ready to do something about it. Quinn looked him in the eye and nodded.

"How does one go about starting a revolution?" she asked.

Wade chuckled, lightening his grim look.

"I reckon we'll start by getting off this mountain," he said.

They stood, and he pointed out a ledge to her left and explained how they would go down the rockface. Quinn followed him, copying his movements carefully. As they picked their way down the cliffside, the sun climbed up the sky. The ice was melting from the rocks, making them slippery.

"After we get off the mountain," she said. "What're we doing?"

"Finding an RT," Wade said.

"What're you planning on doing there?"

"I got an idea."

Quinn's brows drew together.

"You see, those people in the RT are all privy to a fact that Citizens aren't. Terra doesn't care about the people. All she wants is to keep everyone complacent and unquestioning. But she's made a mistake. She, for some reason, has not executed those who've failed to meet her requirements. You know what that means?"

Quinn awaited the answer.

"That means you've got whole towns full of miserable, angry people who have been mistreated, but don't quite know it. All they know is something's wrong. They just don't know how to fix it. They don't know that they can!"

He paused.

"I used to be one of them; I know what it's like. But now I also know that things used to be different. It was rough, too, as you and I have seen."

Wade stopped and turned to look at her.

"Think of what a group of angry people can do. A group who's been unknowingly slaves. Anger can be a powerful strength, Missy Quinn."

He paused, thinking. He nearly always did that- thought long and carefully before he spoke.

"I reckon," he continued. "We could talk those people into fighting back."

Quinn nodded. "Worth a shot, I think," she said.

It took several more hours for them to make it down the cliff. The sky was cloudless and the sun bright, but it didn't do much for the cold. Quinn's nose ran, and her fingers felt stiff. She pulled her hands up into her sleeves and then shoved them into her pockets.

Wade suddenly pulled up short, holding out his hand for her to stop. They stood on another ledge, and from there, the mountain seemed to slant downward, tapering off until there was no more mountain. Wade had fixated his eyes on something, but Quinn could not see it.

"What're you looking at?"

Wade pointed at something, far past what she thought was the end of the mountain: a wall, white like the snow and with trees sprouting up all around it. Within it she could barely see the tops of tall buildings.

"What is that?" she asked.

"A City," Wade answered. "We make it there, and we might be able to find our way to an RT."

He turned his head, looking around. He nodded to a ledge.

"We'll go down that way," he said. "It's gonna be harder, though."

Quinn exhaled. "Great."

It was harder and slower than any of the climbing they had yet done, and time dragged by. The sun surpassed the noontime peak, and was soon descending the westerly sky. They stopped to rest at what she judged to be four. Her hands were scraped and chapped, and her body ached from the continuous exertion.

"How're you holding up, Missy Quinn?" Wade said.

"Alright," Quinn answered. "My hands are pretty tore up. It is dang cold out here."

Wade chuckled.

"I suppose you've never climbed anything like this," he said.

"No," Quinn answered. "But everything is so very much realer here."

Wade nodded, his hat bobbing up and down on his head.

"So it is," he said. "Half an hour. Then we move."

He took off his hat and sat down, leaning against the backpack. He pulled out his little book and began reading.

"Whatcha got there?" Quinn asked.

"Psalms," Wade said, glancing up at her.

"You really believe that stuff?"

"Yes."

Quinn was not sure if she did. She'd read out of a big old Bible at the orphanage, and she'd even been to church with the Connors a time or two. But she'd not often seen someone who professed to believe actually do so.

Except Wade. He didn't even have to tell her that he did; she already knew. And that made her consider, more than anything else ever had, that perhaps it really was the truth.

She twiddled her fingers, then asked, "Will you read some to me?"

He lifted his gaze from the page to her eyes. "Sure."

He read a couple chapters aloud, and she listened silently, staring up at the sky; after that, they were off.

By sunset, they were three quarters of the way down. Tomorrow they would finish their descent and make their way to that big walled City. They slept, and in the morning began climbing, down and down and down.

It was cloudy today, and Quinn could smell rain. Just when she was thinking it would not come, it did. Freezing, heavy rain, so dense they could barely see through it. Having no cover, they were soaked as they waited it out. For almost an hour. When it finally stopped, the rocks were so slippery they still could not move.

"At least it didn't snow," Quinn said.

Wade grunted. Quinn shivered, wishing she had fur like the squirrel in the branch across from her. Or fur like Wade's, for that matter. He was blessed with a thick coat of hair all over. He moved closer and draped one side of his big coat over her to garner heat.

Eventually, things dried out enough for them to keep going. By then it was nearly noon again. Wade stopped and grumbled.

"What?" Quinn asked.

"Just...trying to find the next place to go," Wade mumbled.

Quinn looked around. An enormous tree grew alongside them, thirty feet high, with lower branches that spread close to the ground.

"There," she said, pointing to the tree.

"What?" Wade said. "That tree?"

"Mm-hmm," Quinn said. "The branches should be easy to climb down. It'll probably be faster than poking our way down the rockface."

Wade studied the tree. "Alright."

They switched places, and Wade grabbed the closest branch, pulling on it to test its strength. Satisfied, he swung his legs up, wrapping them around the branch. He righted himself on the topside of it, and moved toward the tree trunk. He climbed to the next branch, and the next one. She began her own descent.

Wade dropped to the shelf of rock below as Quinn climbed onto the last branch, measuring her drop to the ground. She was getting ready to jump down when she slipped on a slick bit of bark and fell most ungracefully. She landed on her side, hitting her left shoulder hard.

"You alright?" Wade asked.

Quinn rolled onto her back and attempted a response, which only came out as a distressed exhale.

"Uh-huh," Wade said. "Been there, done that before." He nudged her arm with the toe of his boot. "Glad it was you and not me."

Quinn coughed.

"Ha ha ha," she squeezed out.

He knelt and took her arm, pulling her up to a sitting

position. She focused on breathing, in and out, in and out. Gradually her wind returned, and though her aching was not one that would soon leave, she found she could stand.

"Your shoulder alright?" Wade asked.

Quinn shrugged, which hurt her shoulder terribly. "Yeah," she said.

"Good," he said, inclining his head to the right. "I see a way down that direction. Looks a little easier."

"Great," Quinn said, gladder of that than she sounded. "Let's go."

It was an easier way down, and they had made it to the edge of the mountain. Still being slightly above the wall, Quinn could see the tops of the strange tall buildings.

From the bottom of the cliff, there would be a two- or three-mile trek across a flat expanse to the City's gate. They stood and looked out on it.

"Alright," Wade said. "Let's get down there. Maybe we can make it by tonight."

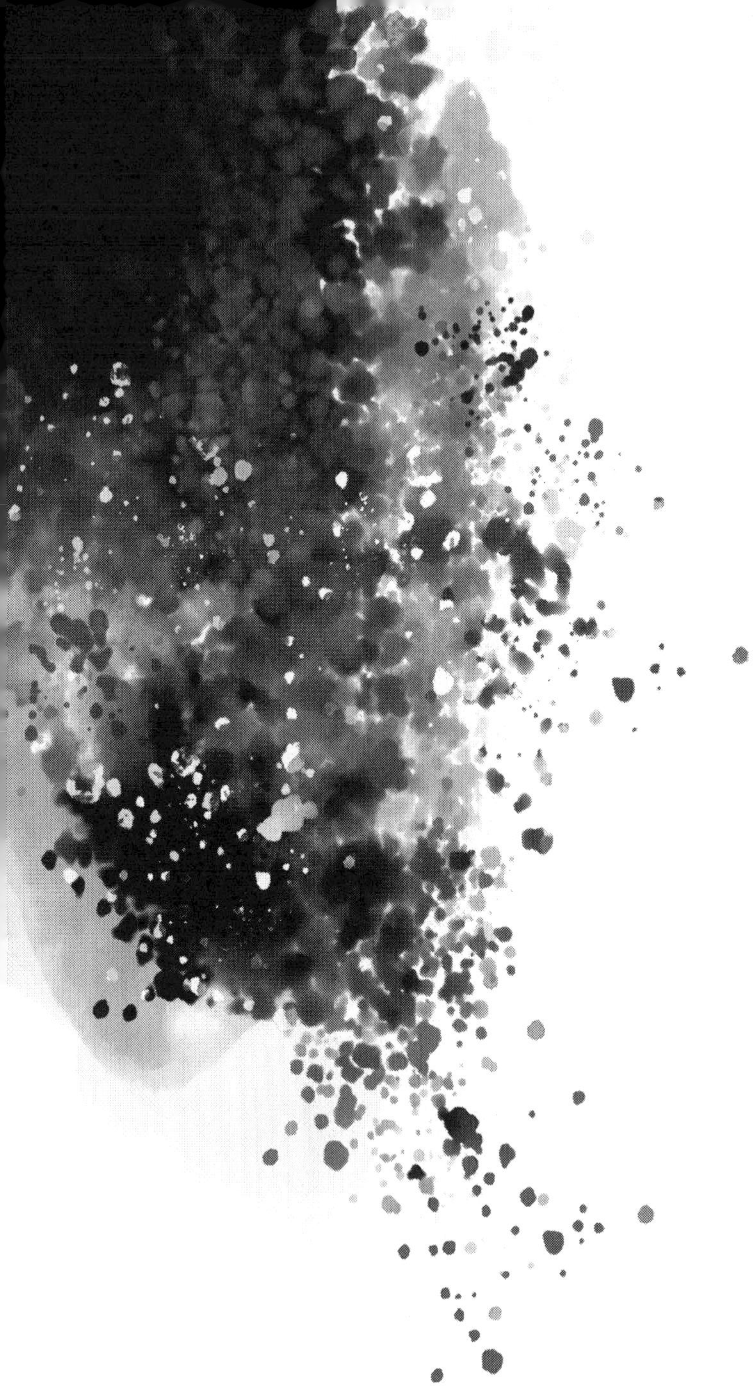

IX

They made it a quarter of the way to the City by dusk. It was difficult to see anything in the odd, dim light; harder than if it had been fully night. Large trees grew sporadically all around them, adding to the darkness.

An eerie feeling pricked his awareness, and his hand went to his gun. He didn't hear anything besides his and Quinn's footsteps and the wind.

Then a momentary commotion, Quinn yelling, and a sputtering which Wade had forgotten until that moment, all as he turned and drew his gun. He could only see the form of the TRACKER in the bad light, but he recognized it instantly: one of the monstrous metal-man hybrids Terra used to guard Cities and hunt people down. He thought this one might be a guard, though he wasn't sure what it was doing this far out.

And it had Quinn. It was dragging her away through the trees.

"Wade!"

He took off. Quinn yelled again, her voice seeped in terror.

"Hang on!" he called.

He couldn't see well enough to shoot it from this distance, not to mention while he and it were moving. He had to get it to stop somehow. Maybe if he could get in front of it... He pushed himself to a full sprint, passing the behemoth monstrosity and stopping in its path. He fired once into the air, and the TRACKER pulled up short.

In the dark, its eyes looked black and lifeless, though he knew that was not so. They were human eyes, those of someone sentenced to mutilation and exterior control of the body, while the mind remained intact but powerless. He'd only seen and heard a TRACKER once before, back in his days in the RT, from a distance.

Quinn squirmed and struggled in its grip, crying out as its talons squeezed her, and the TRACKER leaned its face down to hers, letting out a distorted wail mimicking her own. Wade recoiled at the noise, the freakish imitation of Quinn's terror sending his stomach into knots.

As the TRACKER continued its scream, Quinn thrashed harder, more frantic. One taloned hand was reaching for her throat, and it had forgotten Wade for the moment. If Quinn stopped moving, he'd have a clear shot before it snapped her neck.

"Be still!" he shouted. "Stop thrashing!"

Her wild eyes caught his momentarily. Questioning.

"Trust me, Quinn!"

He took aim. She stopped thrashing- its hand was around her neck- he fired- the TRACKER's head snapped back with a spray of blood and mechanical components. It fell to the ground, taking Quinn with it.

Wade rushed forward and knelt beside Quinn, prying the still fingers away from her neck. As soon as he'd gotten her free, she stumbled a few feet away, wrapping her arms around herself. Wade put another bullet in the monster's head, then walked over to the girl. She shook vehemently, and he could hear muffled sobs from beneath the hand covering her mouth.

He gently tried to take her arm and steady her, but her whole body bristled at the touch. "Quinn…"

"Sorry," she said, her voice hoarse.

This time with a firmer hand, he put an arm around her shoulders and made her face him. Her cheeks were wet, her eyes darting, her mouth quaking.

"Just breathe," he said, putting his other arm around her. Her sobs shook her whole body, but he held her steady. When she finally began to calm down, he eased her to the ground, keeping one arm around her.

"What…was that thing?" she asked, voice cracking.

"It's called a TRACKER," Wade told her.

"Its eyes," she said. "It had…human eyes."

"There was a human in there," he said, slowly. "They took him apart and put him together again, and preprogrammed his body from the outside."

"And it…it was copying me," she stuttered. "It used my voice." A shiver rippled through her spine. "I thought I was gonna die."

"I wasn't going to let that happen."

Quinn inhaled and exhaled, slowly, calming herself. They sat like that a few more minutes. Wade reloaded his revolver.

"We need to get going," he said. "Sooner or later they'll find that body, and we better be gone by the time they do."

Quinn nodded. Wade stood, then pulled her up. He led her back the way they'd come, carefully avoiding the body.

It was still dark a couple hours later when they approached the City's gate. Above the closed gate, there was a large placard which read C-3. Wade peered around.

He started to the left of the gate, poking around for anything that would give him an idea of how to get in.

Finally, he spotted something on the wall. When he drew close enough to see that it was a series of small divots, cut into the side of the wall, he said, "We can climb this."

"But how to get down once we reach the top?" Quinn asked, her voice still tremulous.

"We'll see when we get there," he said.

Quinn raised her brows but did not say anything.

Wade pointed to the ladder. "You first."

He stepped back and she began climbing up. He worked his hands into one of the divots, then his right foot. It was not much harder than climbing a ladder, though he did not think that that was its purpose. It seemed more of a decorative sort of thing.

When they finally reached the top, which was about six feet wide, they sat for a moment, looking down into the silent City. The streets were empty; no one was out. Wade looked at the entrance. There, two guards were posted, each in a little hutlike structure on either side of the gate.

"It's so strange," Quinn said. "All the buildings are so close together. How can anyone breathe?"

"It is a wonder," Wade replied. "But they've never known anything else. It's normal to them."

Though it was dark, he could see apartments, a few houses, swimming pools, a tennis court, a couple restaurants and some offices. A government building, and a law enforcement complex.

When he had lived in one of these, it was never so quiet at night. People still did things. Perhaps they had instilled a curfew since his childhood in the City.

"Look," Quinn said.

She stood and walked along the wall rightward. She stopped and pointed to a nearby building. It was close enough to the wall that they could probably jump down onto its roof. Wade stood and walked over to her.

"This plan greatly resembles the tree one," he said. "A fall from this would have much less happy results."

"I'm not gonna fall," Quinn retorted.

He was glad to see the snark return; she was recovering from the attack. She backed to the edge of the wall, took off, and leapt, her long duster coat flaring out around her as she descended to the rooftop. She made it, barely.

Wade prepared for his jump, walking to the edge as she had, sprinting from there. His jump was a much less dramatic affair; it was more of a step, as his longer legs didn't require a grand leap to make it.

There was a stairwell on the roof. Wade walked over to it, trying the doorknob. It turned and he opened the door. Quinn followed him inside. They started down the stairs. At the bottom stood a door. This one was locked, but had a glass window.

Wade withdrew his revolver and ordered Quinn back up the stairs a bit. He reared back and smashed the window with the butt of his gun, sending shards of glass in all directions. Making sure his sleeve covered as much of his hand as it could, he reached into the hole and found the door's lock. A loud siren began wailing. Quinn covered her ears.

"What is that?!" she demanded.

"We've set off an alarm," Wade said, pulling his arm back in and opening the door. "Come on."

He turned this way and that, trying to get a feel for what sort of place they were in. Nearby, he saw an old gurney and some medical machines. This was a hospital.

"What are those?" Quinn asked, her voice nearly drowned out by the siren.

"Ahm," Wade said, unsure as to how he would explain what a heart monitor was to someone who had spent most of her life in the past.

He just grabbed her arm and pulled her along. There, another stairwell. He flung open the door and they rushed down the stairs, where they ran into a small man wearing a white lab coat.

"What are you-" he began, but Wade had pistol-whipped him before he had a chance to finish.

Wade pulled off his duster and stuffed it into the pack, then took the man's white lab coat. He pulled it on. The sleeves were tight and it was terribly short, but it would do.

"Take off your coat and hat," Wade said.

Quinn quirked her brow.

"They're too conspicuous," he said.

He had not thought of this before. Their clothing would be exceedingly odd to the Citizens. She slid out of her coat and added it to the large pack. He took each of their hats and squished them in as well.

They rushed down the stairs, leaving the man behind. When they reached the bottom of that stairwell, there was no door. It simply opened directly into this floor. Here, there were hospital rooms on all sides. He could hear screaming coming from one of them, despite the ever-loud sirens.

Suddenly, an armored individual burst out of one of the rooms, prodding a pale, pain-ridden man forward with a baton.

"Everyone out!" the man in armor shouted. "We are evacuating the building! Out!"

Wade scooped Quinn up into his arms, getting an idea. She weighed a lot more than he would have thought she did.

"What're you-" she spouted, but he interrupted.

"Look sick," he said.

"What?" she asked.

"Look sick! Pretend you aren't feeling well," he instructed. "Like when we first got here."

Finally catching on, she dropped her head, letting it hang over his arm. She scrunched her face, as if in pain.

"You!" the armored man said, taking notice of them. "Come on. There is an intruder in the building. Get out of here!"

Wade hurried after the man, rounding a corner. There was a line of doctors, nurses, and patients, each waiting for their turn on one of the three elevators. Those who could were going down another stairwell nearby. Wade made for that.

Being careful not to knock any of the tremulous patients over, he weeded his way through the stream of people. Through five more floors and stairwells they went. It seemed that the building was, rather than wide and having one or two floors, tall and ridiculously narrow. The little area each floor possessed was made up for in an abundance of them.

Finally they made it to the bottom floor. Wade slid in amongst the mass of people, keeping his head down. The group made its way outside, and he slipped away from them, setting Quinn down toward the rear of the building. He straightened, stretching his back.

"Goodness gracious, how much *do* you weigh?"

She shrugged and shook her head. Wade slipped off the white lab coat, which he noted had torn through the armpits.

"Now where do we go?" Quinn asked.

"Nowhere tonight, I reckon," he said. "Things seem a little different since I lived in a place like this. We'll just find somewhere to hide out for tonight."

They walked away from the medical facility, toward another building. Wade was not sure what it was. There was nowhere for them to hide behind that one, so they moved on. It was slightly warmer down here, off the mountain. But not much. He pulled their coats out of the bag and they slipped them on.

They moved on, finally finding a small shed three buildings down from the hospital. Wade investigated the shed first, finding it only housed an accumulation of clothing and food. They settled in a corner, behind a large shelf. After poking around the shed for a couple minutes, he found two blankets among the stock and tossed one to Quinn.

"Where're we going tomorrow?" she asked, followed by a long yawn.

Wade thought for a moment. What would they do? Get themselves arrested and hope that they were taken to an RT and not killed?

What criteria did the crime have to meet? Lack of genetic purity. Nearly all the individuals sent to RTs were those considered genetically useless. He was confirmed to have an undesirable trait. Could he somehow pose as a younger man and go to be tested?

He didn't think he could pass for an eighteen-year-old. He tried to remember what he had looked like at eighteen. He had been very thin, having filled out in his twenties. His skin had been paler. He cringed when he remembered his attitude then; he'd been an angry, mean sort, from his teens onward. It seemed those traits had diminished over time, and since Retrospect.

He revisited his memory of the day he'd been tested. They had simply taken a blood sample, and results had arrived three days later. He was subsequently...abducted -that word seemed to fit it best- from his apartment home, and recalled losing consciousness, then regaining it in the RT.

Wade glanced over at Quinn, who had fallen asleep with a furrowed brow. He rubbed his forehead and sat down, pulling the second blanket over his legs. He would find a way to that RT.

X

Quinn woke with a jerk the next morning. She'd spent the whole night running from screaming metal monsters with human eyes; her dreams would be torturous for a long time, she thought.

Wade was not there. She kicked off her blanket and stood, looking around. She walked through the storage room, hunting for Wade. She found him examining one of the shelves.

She asked what he was doing, and in reply he tossed her a wad of cloth. She separated it into light grey pants and a blue shirt.

"To blend in," he said. "I've got a plan."

Quinn walked around the little building for a few moments before finding a secluded spot. She shed her own clothes and donned the strange new ones, arching her back to better see how they looked. The pants were tight, clinging to her bottom and flaring around the calves. Her rear end was very much on display, and it made her slightly uncomfortable. The shirt fit better, she supposed, though it was unlike anything she had ever worn before. The material was strangely smooth and felt cool against her skin.

She walked back into the open area of the shed. There, Wade had changed his clothes to some similar to hers, though his pants were a charcoal color and his shirt was green. She laughed.

"You look ridiculous," she said.

He shrugged and offered a smile.

"The real world prefers comfort to practicality," he said. He frowned. "Well, that won't work."

"What?" she asked.

"Those clothes. Gotta make you look like a boy, somehow," he said.

She squinted. "Huh?"

someone

"Gotta make you look like a boy," he repeated.

She frowned and asked, "Why?"

"My plan," he explained. "Is to get you tested, but not really, so we can get to an RT."

She twisted her mouth as she thought that over. "Tested?"

He nodded. "For undesirable traits. That's a confirmed way to get sent out to an RT. But we don't know if you have any, so we'll somehow switch it with my blood, as we know that I do."

"Why do I have to dress up like a boy?" she said.

"The blood test will show that the blood belongs to a man," he said. "And I can't pass for an eighteen-year-old. Though I'm not certain it's much more likely for you to pass as a boy."

Especially with the clothes he'd found. She'd have to find some baggier, boxy clothing. And do something with her hair, too.

"Where's your knife?" she asked.

Wade retrieved the bag and fished the hunting knife from inside. She quickly re-braided her dark hair, then turned around, pointing to the base of her skull where he should cut it off. He took the braid in one hand and sawed the hair off with the other. What was left quickly pulled loose.

She shook her head and her hair spread out into curly waves. She ran her hand through it and bit the inside of her cheek, momentarily regretting the loss of her locks.

She walked off silently to where Wade had found the clothes. There, she found a larger black shirt and pants. Returning to the area she'd changed in before, she pulled the black shirt on over the blue one. She put on her own trousers, but loosened her belt so they rested low on her hips. Finally, she stuffed her legs into the soft gray pants. That helped.

Now for the really hard part. She searched around the shed, hunting for something to wrap around her chest. Finally, she found a strip of linen bandages. She returned once more to the secluded area of the shed. It took a few minutes, but she got it to work. Somehow.

Her curves concealed and her hair short, she knew she still did not look like a boy.

someone

She returned to where Wade stood waiting. She spread her arms out, turning in a circle. Wade shook his head.

"If we pull it off right, I think we can make it work. The people here won't want to hurt your feelings by telling you you're a girly-looking boy."

Quinn tilted her head in question, then simply nodded.

"Now what?" she asked.

"Now we head over to that hospital, and see what we can do to get ourselves rejected," he told her.

They exited the shed and snuck around the building to the road. Quinn made an effort to walk like a boy. She thought about how Andy walked and tried to imitate his easy-going gait.

"What in the world are you doing?" Wade asked, peering at her.

Quinn grumbled.

"You think that's how men walk?" he said.

"This was your idea," she snapped.

It only took a few minutes to reach the strange, narrow hospital building. Inside what Wade referred to as the waiting room, he had her stop by an elevator while he walked up to a nearby desk. He spoke quickly to the woman behind it.

"I am here to get my son tested," he told her.

He spoke in a strange manner, as she had heard other people here speak. They used no contractions, and all their words were clipped, precise. Wade conferred with the lady for a couple more minutes, then returned to her.

"Your name is Thomas," he said.

"Huh," Quinn said.

The woman behind the counter was looking at her quizzically. Quinn made a point of looking back at her, and the woman averted her eyes upon being caught.

"Don't they need some higher form of verification?" she asked.

"They're overconfident in their system," Wade told her. "They don't think anyone could ever breach it."

"But we already have," she said.

"Doesn't seem like they're letting that get out," Wade said. He paused for a few moments. "Try not to talk too much."

She quirked her brow.

someone

"If you have to, make sure you aren't using any contractions. Try to talk..." he began.

"Like I am a freak who does not have a mind of her own?" she finished, putting stress on her monotone.

"Yeah," Wade said. "They call it Standard. You got it."

They fell silent for a few minutes.

"How are we going to switch our blood samples?" Quinn asked, practicing her Standard.

"All they do is take some of your blood with a needle," he explained.

She cringed. After the experience on the rocket, she wasn't excited about needles.

"Right before they take your blood, pretend to pass out."

"Pass out," she repeated. "How many times do you think they can fall for the fake-sick ruse?"

Wade shook his head and scowled in irritation. "It works. While they express concern over you, I'll take my own blood. Then we convince the doctor that he already took yours."

Quinn frowned.

"But he'll know he didn't," she said.

"Two people's word against his," Wade said. "Haven't you ever thought you did something but everyone else swore you didn't, or the other way around? We convince him that's what happened."

Quinn's whole life she'd thought something and everyone else had sworn it wasn't so. Perhaps it wouldn't be that hard. So they sat and waited. And waited. An hour later, she heard her false name called by an echoey, bored voice. They stood, and walked up to the counter.

XI

Wade sat in a chair in the exam room. Quinn sat on the table while Dr. March, a young, blonde-haired man with brown eyes and plenty of extra weight, prattled on about the societal recompense of genetic testing.

He had a shape akin to a rotund chicken; mass abounding on the top half of the body, cut into by a tight waistband, and tiny twigs for legs. He defied gravity. How could such little legs hold up such an enormous top half?

Dr. March asked Quinn a few simple questions about her health, which she vaguely answered. The man spoke in a sluggish manner, as if he was trying to ensure that she understood him. Wade thought he was trying to make sure he understood himself. When he had finished his speech, the doctor left the room to retrieve his equipment.

Wade glanced up at Quinn, who crinkled the sanitary paper covering the table with her fingers. She truly looked nothing like a boy.

But, as he had predicted, no one said anything. The Citizens of Terra were taught not to criticize or tease their peers, as he now remembered. He'd often had a hard time with that one.

Roughly a minute later, Dr. March returned and stood beside the exam table. He took Quinn's arm and turned it over to extract the blood from her vein. Quinn swayed slightly.

"Are you alright, Thomas?" asked the doctor.

Quinn nodded, then affectedly rolled her eyes upward and allowed herself to fall backward.

Thunk!

Her head struck the wall behind her. Wade saw her scrunch her nose in pain for a moment before assuming a look of placid unconsciousness. Dr. March gasped, let the needle fall to the exam table, and stood for a moment, registering what just happened.

Wade jumped up and stood by the table. Feigning concern for Quinn, he grabbed the syringe and found his vein. He inserted the needle and waited for it to fill, glancing up at Quinn, who groaned loudly. Once he'd drawn enough blood, he returned the needle to where it had fallen. He pressed a finger to the puncture.

"Thomas? Can you hear me? Quick-" Dr. March turned to Wade. "Go get one of the nurses to help."

Wade nodded but tarried a few more moments. Quinn slowly opened her eyes.

"Oh, there you are. Are you alright, Thomas?" Dr. March asked.

Quinn nodded.

"He does not like needles much," Wade said.

After ensuring that Quinn was completely alright, Dr. March said, "We can wait a few days to try again, if you feel more comfortable with that."

"But, doctor, you already took her- uh, his blood," Wade said.

Dr. March picked up the blood-filled syringe. The man

turned it over in his hands, looking from it to Quinn. He frowned.

"But I..." he stuttered. "I could have sworn I did not take it."

Wade chuckled amiably. "It happens to the best of us," he said. "In the excitement, it must have left your mind."

"I suppose so," Dr. March finally yielded.

March laughed. Wade laughed. Quinn laughed. They stopped laughing.

"Well, you are free to go, then," Dr. March said, scratching his head. "Your results will be in by tomorrow. Come back in at 1300."

Tomorrow? They were faster than when Wade had been tested. But, all the better for them, he supposed. Quinn slid off the exam table.

"Please, take it easy for the rest of the day," Dr. March said.

"Do not worry. I will make sure he does," Wade said.

They left the room, and quickly made their way out of the hospital building. They returned to the storage shed to hide out until the next day. Wade settled down on one of the blankets while Quinn changed out of her "boy clothes" at the other end of the shed.

When she returned, she lay down across from him and closed her eyes. Wade reclined as well. The day dragged on, but they needed the rest after their long trek.

Wade pondered what to do with their guns. Leaving them behind was out of the question. Maybe he could disassemble them, and they could hide the pieces on their persons.

It was the only thing he could think of, so he poked around the shed until he found a small screwdriver. Then he set about his work, praying nothing broke.

He managed to separate the barrel from the cylinder and handle. The biggest piece was the barrel. He'd have to stash that in his boot. He also found two small bags, and put as many bullets as he could inside them. Gently, he nudged Quinn awake so he could take her gun apart too.

"They won't search us?" she asked.

"I doubt it," Wade said. "I had earbuds in my pocket when they took me before. I remember waking up and them being there, fully intact."

"Ear-whats?"

"Never mind. I don't think they'll search us. They don't believe anyone can breach their security."

"If you say so."

The following day, around noon, Wade and Quinn prepared to leave. They ate food they'd found in the shed. Quinn did whatever it was she did to make herself look like a boy, and Wade made sure that they each had all the pieces of their weapons safely hidden. He took his little Bible out of his pocket and slipped it into his boot, beside his gun barrel. Quinn wedged the ammo bags into her own boots.

They wore their old clothes under the Terrian ones, and their coats over that. Wade carried the now-flat backpack, empty except for their crushed hats and holsters, under his coat. The jackets would still be out of place, but not like their full Retrospect ensembles.

They left the shed and walked to the hospital. In the waiting room, things felt strange to Wade, like when it is about to storm, and all the animals and bugs outside go quiet. The woman behind the counter, a different one from yesterday, stared at them.

"Thomas at 1300?" she asked.

Wade nodded. She stood.

"Follow me, please," she said.

She walked around the counter and led them through an unmarked doorway. Wade glanced down at Quinn, who looked slightly apprehensive. She met his eyes and raised her brows. He patted her shoulder before turning back to study their surroundings. It was an empty hallway, with strange yellow lights stationed on the ceiling every five feet. The lights cast an odd glow, making their skin look sickly and yellow.

Finally, they came to a door on the right side, and the woman stopped. She knocked, and it opened before she had even drawn her hand back. She motioned them inside. The room was empty, save for a small table and a few metal chairs.

The lights inside were austerely bright, and left nothing in shadow. Dr. March stood at one end of the table, and an older man with black hair stood nearby. The black-haired man wore an armor/coat hybrid, which Wade recognized as being the attire of an Enforcer. The man had come to haul them off. His plan had worked.

Dr. March pointed to the chairs, seeming slightly nervous. Wade and Quinn each sat down. Dr. March spoke, while the other man remained silent.

"We have received the results from Thomas's test," said Dr. March. He narrowed his eyes, his fat chins quivering. "It has been determined that he possesses an undesirable hereditary trait, which renders that he be placed in an RT to prevent the continuance of the trait in future Terrian offspring."

Wade remembered hearing this exact same spiel when he had come before.

"And by determining this, it is also known that you, Thomas's father, must also possess the trait. Therefore, you are to be sent also."

They were disgusting. And he was using it against them. The man with the black hair finally moved. He walked over to their side of the table, smirking. Before Wade or Quinn could react, the man had injected them simultaneously with two large needles. Everything went black.

XII

Quinn woke up on something hard. She spread her hands over it quickly. It was a cot. She sat up, opening her eyes. She was in a small, empty room. It was dirty, and the cracked walls were painted a sad grey color. She still wore her boy clothes, and she could feel the pieces of disassembled revolver in her boot and under her shirt. There was a single window, and there stood Wade, gazing out. He looked over his shoulder and regarded her waking.

"We made it," he said. He turned back to the window. "This is where they brought me before. It's the same RT."

He seemed in a state of wonder. Quinn was just glad they had made it without their things being discovered.

Wade was right about them being overconfident in their system. It was a terrible weakness. They didn't even verify identities before shipping them off.

Overconfident and incompetent.

She took out the gun components and ammo, giving them to Wade. He sat down on the floor and began putting their guns back together.

"Do normal people know about these places?" she asked.

"Citizens? Yes," Wade said. "I can recall, before I came here myself, occasional news coverage of RTs. They would show clips on television of people being arrested and taken here for incompliance."

"Television?" Quinn asked.

Wade gave a snort/exhale. "You'll see one for yourself eventually."

Quinn shrugged, then voiced a thought, "If the...Citizens...are so well taken care of and placid and happy, why show them RTs at all? Why ruin the illusion?"

Wade considered that.

"Fear," he said. "Keeping people afraid keeps them in

line."

"And then," Quinn said. "Why any of it? Why not just enslave everyone?"

Again Wade considered that for a moment. "Now that, I'm not so sure about. I've wondered that too. I reckon that perhaps the Legislators -the ones in charge- want to have an actual society. Maybe that's where some of the discrepancies come from."

Quinn stood up from the bed and walked over to the window.

"So what do people do here?" she asked.

"They run rampant with what they can get. Food rations are shipped in, and it's a free-for-all to get some. There can be bartering for it with people who get more. Or you could steal some. Maybe sell yourself or someone else for it."

"Is there any kind of law?"

"There are guards, but they leave people to their own devices unless someone's really trying to escape."

He handed over her six-shooter while holstering his own, then pulled on the backpack. He pointed to a door near the end of the bed.

"Bathroom," he said.

Was that what they called an outhouse in the real world? The word sounded familiar. She entered the small room, closing the door behind her.

You'd think it'd be called an "in-house," she thought, seeing how it's inside.

Against one wall there was a small sink with a big mirror, and on the other wall a strange white contraption. She walked to the white thing and examined it. She lifted its lid. There was a sort of bowl, full of water, and a handle on the side.

She pondered its use. Seeing how this was the real-world equivalent of an outhouse, and there was no chamber pot or hole in the floor, the thing must have been the device used for defecation.

Shaking her head, she went back to the mirror, and studied her reflection. She had not often seen herself in a mirror. Her short hair curled at the ends around her ears.

She smirked at the thought of those imbeciles believing her to be a boy. It was ridiculous. If she had tried that back home, she would have been ridiculed and declared insane-

or, more insane.

She slid out of the large boys' pants she'd had on over her own, but kept the soft Terrian shirt. She exited the bathroom and gave Wade a nod. They left the room, going through a hallway and down a stairwell.

At the bottom, Wade pushed open another door, and they came into a lobbylike room. There was a desk at one side, similar to the one at the hospital, but no one sat behind it. Quinn glanced over and found that Wade was already heading toward the exit. She trotted after him.

He pushed the door open and cold air rushed in, blasting her face. She looked around, blinking in the bright daylight. The street was narrow like the buildings sandwiching it, as well as unpaved. The tight proximity of the buildings made her feel claustrophobic.

Wade was going to the left. She followed him. He seemed to know where he was going. Really, he looked determined. She wondered just where it was he was heading.

As they walked, she only saw a few people around. Bedraggled, sad-looking people. They passed by a parklike area, with a few large oak trees that would be easy to climb.

At the top of one, there was an especially large spot that resembled a platform, perfect for at least two people to sit on. She noticed a ragged rope tied around the trunk, its end flailing in the wind.

She realized she had fallen behind Wade again, and hurried to catch up. They turned into an alleyway at the other side of the park.

Two of those tall, skinny buildings rose up on either side. Three people would not be able to walk side by side through here. Dr. March would not have been able to walk through here at all. That almost made her laugh, imagining the doctor attempting to get through this alley.

Finally, Wade stopped. There was a window to their right, and he carefully slid his fingers under the pane and lifted it. He climbed inside, turned, and pulled her up and in.

Quinn looked around. She could not see anything; the light coming through the window did nothing to illuminate the rest of the place. It was an odd effect. She reached out and caught Wade's arm, holding on to it as they made their way forward. Her shin bumped into something. A stair.

someone

Wade started up the stairs, and she followed carefully. At the top, Wade stopped. His sleeve felt different than it had before. She waited, and opened her mouth to ask him what they were doing.

Suddenly, a bright light flashed on, blinding her. When her vision returned moments later, she glanced up at Wade; it wasn't him. She let out a yell and stumbled away from the thin, blonde man, who looked almost as surprised as she was.

"Quinn!" Wade hollered from below.

Quinn fumbled her way to the stairs and ran down them, tripping on the penultimate one. This was going to *hurt*... Someone grasped her arm before she fell. Wade hoisted her back up and she latched onto his arm. She was embarrassed at her reaction, but her heart pounded furiously and her legs quaked. She wasn't letting go.

"Hey, who are you?" asked a voice from the top of the stairs. The blonde man.

"Kenneth?" Wade asked.

He repeated, with a sharper tone, "Who are you?"

"Wade," Wade answered.

"Wade Walker?" the man, Kenneth, asked surprisedly after a few moments of silence. "But you were...what are you doing here? How are you here?"

Wade began ascending the stairs, and Quinn finally let go of his arm and followed. She squinted again in the bright light, this time taking in the surrounding room.

It was empty, save for two small cots on the floor, a table, and some strewn-about clothes. She turned her eyes back to the Kenneth man. He looked a bit younger than Wade. His skin was smoother, but he had more grey in his already light-colored hair. The man stared at Wade.

"What are you doing here?" he asked again, a dark look crossing his face. "After what happened with Addi, I never thought I would see you again. And I was glad of it." He talked like all the other Terrians: stiffly, with no contractions. "She loved you."

Kenneth took a swing at Wade's head and Quinn jumped in surprise. It was a terrible one and Wade could have easily evaded it, but he didn't. It grazed his left ear. What was the man's problem? What was he talking about?

He pulled back his fist for another punch, but this time

Quinn drew her revolver.

As -annoyingly- always, she dropped it, but had it back in her hand and trained on the man just as fast. He stopped, staring at her gun.

"What..." he stuttered.

He squinted at the weapon, trying to decide what it was.

"Back off," Quinn snarled. "Or I'll take your head off."

Kenneth stared at her. He took a step forward. She cocked the revolver. He stopped. Wade turned and looked at her.

"It's alright, Quinn," he said quietly. "Put that away."

Begrudgingly, and never taking her eyes off Kenneth, she did as he said. Once her revolver was holstered, she crossed her arms over her chest, waiting. Kenneth glared at Wade.

"What are you doing here?" he asked again. "Who is she?"

"She's Quinn," Wade said. "We escaped..." He paused, twisting his mouth in thought.

"Escaped?" Kenneth spat. "You escaped the City?"

Wade frowned at the man. "City?" he repeated.

Kenneth's fists clenched at his sides. "You sold out Addi to get back into your City," he said. "Do you know what they did to her after you left?"

"I didn't go back there," Wade said. "I made a deal with them: after my trial, I agreed to become a part of an experimental project, and they said they'd leave her alone."

Kenneth stared.

"I do not believe you. They said you agreed to give her location if you could get back to your City," he stated.

"They lied," Wade answered. "You know I wouldn't do that."

"Do I?" Kenneth asked. "I have found in this place that I cannot trust anyone or anything. Your leaving being a major factor."

"He's telling the truth," Quinn said.

She could vouch for the Operation Retrospect part, though she had no idea about the other things they were talking about. Kenneth narrowed his eyes at Quinn.

"I did not ask you, girl," he spat.

Now it was Wade's turn to throw a haymaker. Kenneth did not stand a chance. The man went down like skinny tree in a hurricane. His nose began gushing, and a few tears squeezed out of his eyes. Wade rubbed his fist with the opposite hand.

"You don't talk to her that way," Wade said, glaring down at the man. "I know we used to be friends. I imagine neither of us are the same men we were then." He paused. "But I came back here to try and do something about this whole thing, and I came to you first to see if you would help me. Did I make a mistake?"

Kenneth stared up at Wade. Finally, he sighed.

"Alright, Wade. Just start at the beginning, will you?" he asked.

Wade nodded, and extended his hand to Kenneth. The man took it and stood up, holding his injured nose. He waved them over to the cots on the floor, and they all sat down; Quinn and Wade on one, Kenneth on the other.

Wade glanced at Quinn. He held up his left hand, tapping the thin metal ring with his thumb. For the first time, she realized its purpose.

"I had a match after all," he said, to her. "Just not one made by Terra."

He turned to Kenneth, and started at the beginning. Her name was Addi. Their union -unrecognized by Terra- had brought along a new someone; unacceptable for two denied family.

"They found me and took me in. Beat me senseless."

That hurt she'd first noticed on the side of the cliff was the only thing in his eyes now. Her throat felt tight as she imagined remembering a lifetime all at once. Remembering *this* all at once.

"She was hidden in town, and I was the only person who knew where she was. When I came to, they took me into a sort of courtroom. Someone detailed the accusations against me. There was no way I was getting out, but Legislators offered me a deal to save them."

Them. Addi, and Wade's baby.

"I agreed that if I would be a part of Terra's new project, they would be safe."

He was subsequently shipped off to the moon, stripped of his memories, and inducted into the simulated historical setting. Thence came the story of Retrospect, and how Quinn fit into the picture. Kenneth listened intently, asking no questions, until Wade was finished.

"They did not..." the man began. "They did not let her go free, Wade." His eyes flicked around. "They knew where she was. They found her, and they took her into the clinic. They said that you gave up her location and returned to your City."

Quinn could not see Wade's face, as it was turned toward Kenneth, but she could see his jaw tense up. He stood, stalked to one end of the room, facing away from them. Quinn could tell he was struggling to keep it together. A few moments later he walked back to the cots.

"Is she..." he began, looking at Kenneth intensely. "Is she still here?"

Kenneth nodded slowly. "She lives down the street from here. I take her food and supplies sometimes."

"Let's go," Wade said.

Kenneth stood. "I do not know if..." he said.

"Now," Wade said, with a quiet, unnerving intensity which startled Quinn.

Kenneth nodded and crossed the room, going back down the stairs. Wade followed, and then Quinn. She swiped at her eyes as she trailed after them, praying -for the first time in her life- for Wade.

XIII

As he followed Kenneth back out into the alleyway and down the street, Wade's mind raced. He was going to see her again. What she must think of him...they told her he'd left, sold her out. And Terra had killed their baby. He had thought that he might actually have a child out there somewhere.

But that had been illogical. He ought to have known better- they wouldn't honor a deal with him, and no one else would know the difference. He dragged a hand across his eyes.

Help me, he prayed.

What was he going to say to her?

Give me something to say.

They were out on the main street. Kenneth was headed for one of the tall apartment buildings.

Help me.

Kenneth stopped in front of the building. He opened the front door, and Wade and Quinn followed him in. They walked to a stairwell on the opposite side of the room and began the ascent.

Two flights up, Kenneth pushed open a door which led to a hallway. Doors lined the walls, each with a number. Eight. Nine. Ten. They stopped before Eleven. Kenneth knocked on the door. Wade's heart knocked on his ribcage.

They waited a couple minutes. Kenneth knocked again. Wade heard shuffling from inside. The door opened a crack, stopped by a chain lock.

"Kenneth?" a female voice peeped.

A pair of brown eyes peeked through the crack. The eyes flicked from Kenneth to Wade. They studied him for a moment, confused. The door slammed shut, he heard the lock slide, and it reopened.

There stood Addi, looking so the same and so very

different. She was thinner, her face was lined, her hair streaked with greying strands; she still had her freckles, and her beautiful brown eyes, and her intense stare.

She was his, he was hers- that was why he'd never removed the metal band from his finger, even when he couldn't remember its purpose.

"Addi?" Wade whispered.

She stared at him a few moments more, uncomprehendingly. Then her look changed. Recognition flicked across her face, then rage. The corners of her mouth dropped, her brows creased, she clenched her jaw. Quinn was eying both Kenneth and Addi, looking unsure of herself.

"You," Addi said.

She stepped out into the hallway, right up to Wade. She shoved a finger at his chest. He stumbled backward into Quinn, knocking her to the floor; she scrambled out of the way.

"You!" Addi yelled. "You left! You left! How could you leave?"

Her voice faltered. She lunged, wrapping her hands around his neck. Her fingernails dug into his throat, choking him out, but he failed to register the pain. He only looked into her eyes, her hatred hitting him harder than anything else could. He wouldn't stop her from doing as she saw fit. The only thing he wanted in the world at that moment was for her hurt to be eased, and if that meant killing him, so be it; apparently Quinn didn't see it that way.

Wade could feel darkness coming, but the pressure suddenly lifted. He coughed, and opened his eyes to see Quinn wrestling Addi away. Kenneth was just stepping in, and tore the two away from each other. Wade sat up, breathing heavy, and glared at the girl.

"Go," he said, his voice dark. "Go on, Quinn."

She looked at him with a question on her mouth. She didn't get it. She didn't understand. Anything.

"Didn't you hear me? Get! Stupid, crazy girl. They were right, weren't they?"

Quinn, staring at him with wide eyes, finally registered what he was telling her. Without a word she stepped past him, her footsteps resounding on the wood floor. He heard a door open and close. Wade dropped his face into one hand. Kenneth stood by, silently. The three of them stayed as they were for several minutes.

"Why did you leave?" Addi finally asked, her voice hoarse. "And tell them where I was?"

Wade lifted his head and looked at her. "I didn't," he said softly.

She turned her sharp eyes on him with contempt. "Explain," she said.

Kenneth decided to leave the two of them alone, walking down the hall after Quinn. Wade leaned against the wall opposite Addi. Her eyes were empty now. Somehow that was worse than the roiling hatred. He inhaled through his aching throat.

"After I was arrested, they offered me a deal. I agreed to be a part of an experiment, and they agreed to let you go free."

"Do you know what they did to me?" she said. "It took weeks for the blood to stop." She inhaled. "Then I was taken back to the clinic. I have not bled since. They do that to all the genetically impure girls now. Sterilize them. I suppose taking us out of Cities was not enough."

She wiped at her face.

"I came to think that you had sold me out," she continued. Her eyes met his, studying, searching. The empty filled with something else entirely. "But I believe you now."

That broke him. He couldn't keep back the tears he'd held in since that night his memories returned. "I'm sorry." His voice cracked. "I'm sorry." He covered his face with his hands, rocking forward.

She took his left hand, fingering the metal band. She reached under the neckline of her shirt, drawing out a string from which hung her own ring.

"I remember when you made these," she said.

He had braided wires from the broken-down RT walls, all those years ago, in his other life, to make these bands.

"It cut your hands, but you insisted."

She broke the string and placed the thin metal circle in his palm, then offered her left hand. Shaking, he slid the band onto her thin fourth finger.

He drew her over to him and they held each other, grieving what, and who, had been stolen from them.

She shifted out of his arms, leaning against the wall

beside him.

"What are you doing here, Wade?" she asked.

He explained Operation Retrospect to her as best he could.

"I would not put it past Terra to do such a terrible thing. But the moon?" she said. She thought for a moment. "That is so absurd it cannot be anything but true."

Wade nodded.

"So it is," he said.

"Who is the girl?" Addi asked.

Quinn.

How could he lose it like that? Must've been shocking, too, because that was more of an old-Wade thing to do. The Wade whom Quinn knew did not do such things. She was impertinent, obstinate and headstrong, with a lot to learn- but she had proven herself to be an exceptional young woman, standing beside him through all of this.

"Quinn," he said. "She's the reason I'm here. She knew, when no one else did, that...where we were...wasn't real. Everyone thought she had something wrong with her."

"As did you?" Addi asked pointedly.

"At first," he admitted. "But now I know she's the only one who didn't."

"She has got a mean fist, too," she said. "I think you better go tell her as much."

He nodded, and stood, taking Addi's hand and helping her up. They headed down the hall to the stairs. In the lobby, Kenneth was seated on a threadbare couch. The man lifted his eyebrows and tilted his head toward the door.

Leaving Addi and Kenneth, Wade crossed to the door and went outside. He looked around. The street was empty. He turned and walked around the side of the building. There he found Quinn, leaning against a wall, arms crossed and face obscured by wild, windblown hair.

XIV

Wade walked over to Quinn and leaned against the wall beside her. She wasn't angry with him for what he'd said. She'd been surprised because she had stopped the woman from choking him to death. But she understood the outburst; understood it all.

"I'm sorry, Missy Quinn," he finally said.

She dismissed it with her hand. She'd rather he forgot it; it probably hurt him more than it hurt her.

"Eh, whatever," she said. "I've heard it a million times before. You used to be one of the only people who'd never said it."

Wade grimaced and dropped his eyes.

"But now you're the only one who's said it but whom I know does not mean it."

His eyes returned to hers. His mouth was slightly upturned.

"Sticks and stones may break my bones..." Wade said.

"But words will tear my heart out," Quinn interrupted.

She looked up at him. He studied her for a moment before concluding that she was joshing him.

"I sort of slipped back into my old self. Since I remembered, sometimes it's hard...sorting out...the me of Terra and the me of Retrospect," he said.

Quinn grimaced. "I'm so sorry. For what they did to you."

She crossed her arms and turned her eyes to the ground, her top teeth biting into her lower lip. Wade tucked one of her roughly-shorn locks behind her ear, angling her face back toward him as he did so.

"It helps me to think," he said, softly. "That he or she may have grown up to be a little like you."

She looked up at him, not sure how to respond.

"As for Terra-Wade and Retrospect-Wade," she said

after a few moments. "The only one that matters is who you are now. The someone you are now has what it takes to take down Terra." She grinned. "Now, is it revolution time yet?"

"I think so," he told her.

"Good," Quinn said.

The two of them returned to the apartment's lobby, where Kenneth and Addi stood. They headed back up the stairs and entered Addi's apartment. The woman took Wade to one of those bathroom things to get something for his throat. Quinn and Kenneth stood in the kitchen, looking at each other.

"How do you know Wade?" Quinn asked the thin man, who rubbed his chin.

"We were brought here around the same time, when we were both eighteen. We have just always sort of known each other," he told her. "I helped Addi after he was gone."

"Did he tell you his plan?" Quinn asked.

Kenneth raised his brows in question.

"He wants to take Terra down," she said.

Kenneth's lips twisted into a sideways-sort-of-smile.

"Finally, I hear something good today," he muttered. "How does he plan to go about this?"

"Ideas are welcome," Wade said, reentering the room, followed by Addi.

Quinn noticed that she had a metal circle around her fourth finger, just like Wade's.

"I think that I have an idea," Addi said, crossing her arms over her chest. Everyone looked at her expectantly.

"Tomorrow is drop-off day," she began.

"Drop-off day?" Quinn asked.

"The day they drop off supplies for us," Addi said. "On drop-off day, we should take advantage of many people being in one place at the same time, and tell them."

She paused.

"I think they will listen. But how do we get it to them? There will be guards around."

"Perhaps we could write something," Kenneth said. "Something to pass out to them."

Wade nodded. "What should it say?" he asked.

Addi retrieved a pencil and paper; she sat down at a small table, which had three chairs. Wade and Kenneth sat in the other two chairs, and Quinn sank down to the floor, listening as they discussed what to write.

"You must start with something that will grab their attention," Kenneth said.

"Terra is evil," Wade said simply.

"That will probably do," Addi said. She scribbled it onto her paper.

"It has perpetrated a long and violent abuse against us, the so-called Citizens of this worldwide nation," Wade continued. "The time has come to question the right of it to do so. The power subduing us ought not be the one ruling us."

Kenneth pitched in: "We must stand, and we must stand together. Are you ready to say *enough*?"

"That covers one-third of the page," Addi said. "I can write smaller, but I think making it bigger better ensures that it will be read. I only have about thirty pages of paper, but we can cut them into three pieces each. That would be ninety."

"That is a good place to start," Kenneth said.

They worked at the message a bit more, and then organized a system. Wade and Quinn divided up the pages into threes; Addi and Kenneth carefully copied the words onto them with pens.

It took a while, but their work was well-rewarded with their message printed on ninety small pieces of jaggedly-cut bits of paper. Once finished, they discussed how they would go about distributing the papers.

They all opted to spend the night at Addi's apartment. A while before bed, Addi motioned Quinn over to the bathroom. There, the woman showed her what she called the shower.

"Like a bath, but much better," Addi told her.

The woman left, closing the door behind her. Quinn turned on the water and adjusted the temperature as Addi had shown her, shed her clothing, and stepped in. It was quite wonderful. She scrubbed her short hair with her fingertips and rinsed all the filth of the last days from her skin.

When she was finished, she shut off the water and stepped out of the tub. She grabbed a towel from the counter and dried herself off. She redressed and exited the room. Addi came up behind Quinn.

someone

"Girls in the bedroom," she said, motioning for Quinn.

Quinn followed her into the tiny bedroom. There was a single cot on one side, and Addi had made up a bed of blankets and pillows for Quinn on the other side.

"Here," Addi said, handing Quinn a very long shirt.

It would reach her knees. Quinn took it back to the bathroom and put it on. It was soft and thin, like the other clothes they had found here. Impractical, but very comfortable. She returned to the bedroom, lay down, and tried to sleep.

After a while, she heard Addi rise and leave the room. Quinn sat up; she could just see into the living room from here. Addi sat next to Wade on her couch. They were talking, but Quinn couldn't understand what they said. She lay back down, listening to the soft, muffled conversation and finally drifting off to sleep.

In the morning, Quinn woke before everyone else. She crept quietly to the bathroom and changed into her own clothes. When she returned, Wade was heading out the door. She followed him to the minuscule porch.

"Good morning," she said.

"Mornin'," he replied.

"When do we go to the…drop-off area?" Quinn asked.

"Think it starts at ten, and it's around eight now, so it won't be long," Wade answered.

He sat down on the top step and took out his little book, as he usually did when he had a minute to himself. She settled herself next to him, and began reading the ninety-first Psalm over his shoulder:

"Thou shalt not be afraid of the fear of the night: nor of the arrow that flieth by day: Nor of the pestilence that walketh in the darkness: nor of the plague that destroyeth at noon day. A thousand shall fall at thy side, and ten thousand at thy right hand, but it shall not come near thee…"

Two hours later the four of them -Quinn, Wade, Addi, and Kenneth- stood in the midst of a small sea of people. They spread through the group, each to a corner.

Everyone faced a big stage-like structure, upon which several men in the coat/armor of the RT guards unloaded boxes from a large vehicle.

Quinn was in the back left corner of the crowd, holding a stack of papers. She separated one from the rest and looked

someone

around. Silently, she placed the slip of paper into the hand of the man next to her, quickly moving away from him. He looked around, scanning the crowd before peering down at the paper in his hand. He turned, and she could not see his face. He tapped the shoulder of a woman next to him and showed the paper to her.

Quinn spread more of the papers, watching for people's reactions. Most had a look of befuddlement as they read it. She saw a few nodding their heads as they read over the page.

Once she had spread all her papers, she carefully made her way to the middle back of the crowd, where they had agreed to reconvene. She spotted Kenneth and hurried over to him. Wade and Addi had not yet returned.

"How'd you fare?" Quinn asked.

"Fine," the man replied. "I saw some nodding heads. Say, why do you talk as you do?"

Quinn peered at him.

"Why do you talk as you do?" she asked in return.

"It is how I was taught," Kenneth answered.

"There you go," Quinn said. "And the way I speak is how

I was taught. Great work figurin' that out."

Kenneth rolled his eyes. Quinn spotted Addi coming toward them, and Wade a little farther off. In a few moments, they were all together again. Quinn felt a hand touch her shoulder. She turned to see a girl her age holding one of their papers.

"Did you see this?" the girl asked.

Quinn shook her head. The girl handed the slip of paper over. Quinn skimmed over it before handing it back.

"What do you make of it?" Quinn asked.

The girl frowned for a moment. "What does it mean, 'are you ready to say enough?'" she said.

"I think," Quinn said, trying to talk like a proper Terrian. "It means something ought to be done about the way things are."

"Who would do it?" the girl said.

"Us," Quinn said. "If not us, then who? Imagine what we could do, if everyone stood together and said 'enough.'"

The girl turned away, thinking that over.

"That is dangerous," she finally said. "Too dangerous." She frowned. "You should not say such things."

Quinn shrugged and walked to the other side of their group, beside Wade.

"Who were you talking to?" he asked.

"Some girl," Quinn said. "She says the message is dangerous."

"She's right," Wade said. "But that's how revolutions go, I reckon."

"And how many revolutions have you started?" Quinn asked.

"Just this one," Wade answered.

"And already you have such wisdom to offer," Quinn said.

Suddenly a loud voice echoed through the crowd. "Everyone line up. Here come your rations," it said.

People scrambled to get in line; there was shoving, shouts, and scuffles all around. Someone pushed Quinn, and Wade grabbed hold of her arm.

"I think we should leave now," Addi said.

"Agreed," Wade said.

They made their way through the throngs back to Addi's apartment.

Three days passed. Addi managed to secure more papers, and they made more slips. They pinned them up strategically throughout the RT: on buildings, on the trees in the center park.

One day, another bit of paper joined one they had tacked to the great big oak tree in the little park. It simply said "*enough.*" It was gradually joined by more and more papers until that oak tree was covered in them up to five feet off the ground. A meeting was arranged. Nearly all the RT people gathered on the fifth night, in an old warehouse which had formerly stored rations.

Quinn stood toward the back of the large room, watching. Anticipation coursed through the air.

Wade's words drifted into her mind, *"Think of what a group of angry people can do."*

Looking out at the group, hearing the reverberation of angry voices, she believed that if they could stand together, they could do something.

Somebody started yelling, and the crowd throbbed. She wheedled her way between people, spotting Addi and Wade at one side and heading for them.

Wade's mouth was pressed into a firm line, and for the first time Quinn thought he looked a little nervous. She took his sweaty hand and he looked down at her.

"We're with you," she said.

He nodded. He and Addi walked to the front of the crowd, leaving Quinn at the side.

Wade got right to the point. He was not shouting, but his voice carried throughout the room. His words, terse and heated by that oft-hidden intensity, resonated. Silence fell over the group and they listened intently.

By midnight, there was a plan.

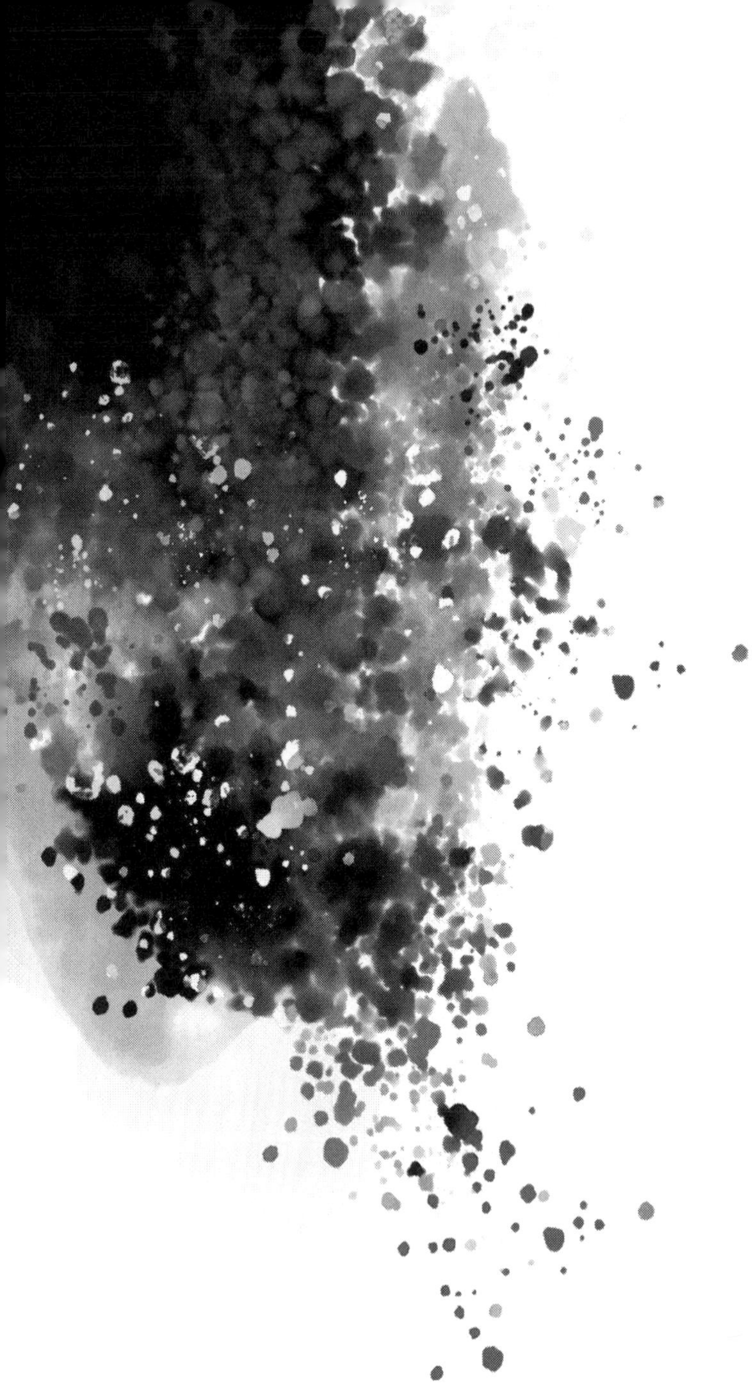

XV

The next morning, Wade sat at the table, fiddling with his gun. Kenneth and Addi had already left to make sure of their preparations.

Quinn was just coming out of the bathroom. Her short hair was damp, and she wore her old clothes: the blue button-down, trousers, and long duster coat.

"You ready?" Wade asked, grabbing their backpack.

Quinn dipped her head and they headed outside together.

"Where do we start?" she asked.

"The first guard post," Wade told her. "We take that, and we secure some weapons for the others. Currently you and I are the only people who have anything close to resembling weaponry. Without some firepower, we'll be done for before we've even started."

They hurried through the town, heading for that first guard post at the entrance. There were four guard posts, and they were the only government presence in town, besides the small clinic. If they took out those posts and the men inside, they controlled the RT. They would plan their next move from there.

When they arrived at the guard post, they made their way to the rear of the building. Wade could see three men at the top of the short tower, keeping watch. Feeble as it may be, there was a stronger guard presence than when Wade had lived here.

Wade and Quinn found the back door; he tried the knob. It was locked, as he'd expected. Beside the door, on the wall, there was a small code panel. One of the men at the meeting had been able to learn the codes for each post, and given them to the respective individuals who were to infiltrate each one.

Wade entered the code and heard a soft click. Quinn

someone

pulled the door open and they cautiously entered the building, walking into what looked like a small breakroom. They crossed into the next room. Wade drew his revolver, and Quinn did the same beside him.

Wade opened the door, and they stepped out into a narrow hallway. To their left was a flight of stairs, which Wade assumed led up to the watchtower. He started up the stairs with Quinn close behind him. Wade slowed when he heard the men at the top talking.

"We run," he instructed Quinn.

She nodded. He held up three fingers. Two fingers. One. They sprinted up the steps into the area atop the tower. Two men stood close together on one side and a third stood on the other side. Wade rushed at the two men standing close together and Quinn at the single one.

The men barely had time to turn before Wade had pistol-whipped one and hooked the other with his fist. Quinn's man had had more time to gather himself, however, and she was wrestling with him. She was losing, and she shot him. As the shot echoed through the RT, he fell backward over the side railing. Quinn looked back at Wade, cringing at the thump of the body.

"You did what you had to," he said.

She nodded, her face grave. He gave the second man a knock on the back of the head with his gun, and took a look at their weapons. They were strange devices, something like guns.

Wade holstered his pistol and picked one up, examining it closely. He pulled its trigger. It launched a small bit of material slowly. When the thing stuck to the wall, it began sizzling with electricity.

"Piece of crap," Wade muttered, but he picked up the other weapon anyway.

Someone else could use them. They hurried back downstairs. In the hallway, a guard was walking away from them. Quinn rushed and pistol-whipped him before he could turn around. He collapsed on the floor. Quinn took his weapon.

They scanned the rest of the building, finding no other guards around. However, they did find a communication room. That was their second objective: find a way to communicate their message outside of the RT. There was an online computer inside with direct communication to the section of Terrian government dedicated to running RTs. Wade noted this. They returned to the breakroom.

"Alright, Missy Quinn," he said. "I'll ensure nobody wakes up. You run and tell the others we've taken the first guard post. And take these."

He handed her two of the four Terrian weapons.

"I'll be back soon," she said. "Be careful."

He looked at her pointedly, said, "You too."

She ran through the back door. Wade returned to the hallway, heaving the unconscious man up onto his shoulder and hauling him up the stairs to the top.

He tied all three of the men to the railing, and searched them for comms and additional weapons. One of them did have a comm device, which began beeping frantically. A screen on the device read "Post 3." Wade answered it.

"Help!" a male voiced screamed from it. "They are taking over-"

Thud!

There was a loud clatter. The man had dropped his comm. Wade heard shuffling and shouts. Then someone else picked up the comm.

"Who is this?" another man said. "Hello?"

Wade recognized Kenneth's voice.

"It's Wade," he answered. "We took Post 1, and Quinn's en route with weapons. Hold on to that comm."

"Alright," Kenneth replied. "We have 3. We have found two weapons. How are they used?"

"Pull the trigger," Wade told him, rolling his eyes. "They shoot little electrical bits. Not quite guns, but they'll do."

"Thanks," Kenneth said. "There is Quinn. I will check back soon."

Wade terminated the call and pocketed the comm. He walked over to the railing, looking over the town. They would soon have all four guard posts. They had taken the Enforcers by surprise; the guards had not been expecting it at all.

He turned and hurried downstairs, back into that communication room. He sat down at the desk in front of the computer he had seen earlier. He rested his fingers on the keyboard, thinking. It had been a long time since he had used one of these.

someone

He took hold of the mouse in his right hand and closed the current window, which was a short report to the Terrian government on how normal things were. He poked around on the computer for a few minutes, keeping his ear attuned to any disturbances.

There was an online browser. He scoured his brain, trying to bring to mind anything he could remember about it. People in RTs had no access to computers. However, he had often used one as a teen in the City.

He clicked the search bar. He found a communication site. Wade typed out their message and posted it anonymously to the top. Then he put it on every other media site he could find. He knew that the sites were fiercely regulated and that his messages would probably be scrubbed in minutes, but somebody out there would see them.

He closed the browser and returned to the watch tower to check on his prisoners. They were still unconscious. His comm beeped, and he answered it.

"We have got 4," Kenneth said. "But I think there is trouble at Post 2. I have sent two men there to keep watch so you can go help 2."

"Alright," Wade said. "I'm going."

He descended the stairs again and walked out the back door. There were the two men, just coming up. He showed them the passcode and started running toward 2. It was not far, and it only took a few minutes for him to reach it. He could hear shouts from inside.

The back door of this one was locked and he couldn't remember the code, so he found a window and kicked it in. He brushed aside the shattered glass and climbed inside.

There was a guard wrestling a young man on the other side of the breakroom. Wade drew his pistol and pointed it at the guard.

"Stop!" he shouted.

The man glanced at him questioningly. He didn't know what the gun was. Wade crossed the room and pulled them away from each other. He shot the guard and searched him, finding another comm device and pocketing it. He would give it to Quinn when he saw her again, so he could keep track of her.

The guard's weapon had ended up by a wall nearby; Wade retrieved it and handed it to the young man, who gapingly stared at the dead guard. Wade showed him how to work the device, and the two of them left the breakroom.

"What's your name?" Wade asked.

"John," the man answered.

Could've guessed that, Wade thought.

Whether he was on earth or otherwise, there was always an abundance of Johns. Wade led the young man up the stairs to this Post's watch tower. There was one guard up there. Wade shot him.

After searching him and finding nothing but the man's weapon, Wade left John at Post 2 and made his way to Post 3. That one was farther away and it took longer for him to reach it. Kenneth was still there, along with four other people.

Wade ordered two of them to head over to Post 2 to help John. Then he headed for 4. When he arrived, he found Quinn and another woman attempting to wrestle something from a girl.

"Hey!" Wade yelled. "What're you doing?"

The woman was surprised by him and momentarily relaxed her hold on the girl, who was able to free her arm.

She wrenched herself away from Quinn in a surprising show of strength and was able to complete the task she was attempting: pressing a button on a comm just like the ones Wade and Kenneth had.

Wade snatched the comm away from the girl as Quinn body-slammed her, taking her down to the ground. Quinn scored a punch to the girl's face before rolling off of her. The girl hissed an unpleasant name at Quinn through clenched teeth. Quinn hit her again.

"Easy, Quinn," Wade said.

She backed away; the girl stayed on the ground. He examined the comm, locating the button the girl had pushed. It was a panic button which would send an alert to authorities of a problem in this RT.

"What'd she do?" Quinn demanded.

"She sent a distress signal to Terrian authorities," Wade answered, then directed his next question to the girl. "Why did you do that?"

"Why would I not?" she snarled. "They sterilized me and sent me here among you people. Maybe now they will allow me back to my City-"

someone

"Terra doesn't play by rules of justice," Wade interrupted. "Don't expect her to repay you."

He looked at Quinn. "Feel free to continue," he said.

Quinn glared at the girl. "She's not worth my bruised fists," she said.

The other woman who had been wrestling the girl had located a rope, and she promptly tied the younger girl's hands and feet.

"Guard her," Wade said to the woman, who nodded her assent.

"What're we going to do?" Quinn asked.

Wade considered her question carefully. He pulled out the comm he'd been using and called Kenneth.

"We've got a problem," he said.

"Of what sort?" asked Kenneth.

"We've just had a girl send out a distress signal," Wade told him.

"Oh," Kenneth said. "That is a problem."

Wade thought for a few moments.

"I don't know what the distress signal warrants from authorities," he finally said. "They could send an army, or one man."

"What do we do?" Kenneth asked.

"Have men at each Post keeping a keen watch on those fronts. On the ground, the air, everything, as far as they can see," Wade said. "Get everyone else together, and make a plan from there."

"Got it," Kenneth replied, and ended the call.

Just then, Wade heard an unsettling sound- a helicopter. He looked up, toward the sound, but could not see anything yet.

"What is that?" Quinn asked.

"A helicopter," Wade answered. "A flying machine. Here-"

He handed her the extra comm and hurriedly showed her how to use it.

"Run to Post 2, and I'll go to 1," he instructed. "This might go downhill fast. Keep that comm handy."

Without a word Quinn took off toward 2. Wade started for 1. His calves were beginning to get sore from all his running.

When he reached 1, he headed straight for the communication room, yelling for the two men he had left there as he went. He had just sat down at the computer desk when they entered the room.

"What is it?" one of the men asked.

Wade quickly explained the situation and instructed one of them to run and tell the others. Wade pulled up the line to the Terrian government. There were two new messages from only ten minutes ago, right after the distress signal.

The first read: "Distress signal received. What is the issue?"

The second had a much more frightening implication.

"Insurrection assumed. Sending authorities now; ETA forty minutes. Kill variables on sight. Abandon RT, shelter in place."

Shelter in place? What were they going to do? Wade stood and called Kenneth again.

"Everyone has to get out of here!" he said. "I think they're going to bomb the town. We've got to get outside."

He yelled to the man in the watch tower, who headed for 3. Wade contacted Quinn and told her. She would tell the others in 2. He then sent a young man to 4. Wade ran for the apartments, where anyone who had not perpetrated their takeover might be. He yelled and yelled.

Finally, one man opened a window in irritation. Wade told him to get anyone who was still inside and to head for Post 4, where there was a back exit. The man ducked inside. Wade repeated this with as many apartment buildings as had people who listened to him.

He herded the group toward 4. They were nearly there when a teenage boy halted in the middle of the street. He tilted his head, listening intently.

"Come on," Wade said.

Then the sound which had first reached the boy's ears reached his. Multiple helicopters.

"Come on!"

They ran the rest of the way to Post 4. He spotted Addi directing people outside of town.

"Where's Quinn?" Wade asked, catching her hand. "And Kenneth?"

"Quinn came through and told me what was happening, but she was circling back around," Addi answered. "I have not seen Kenneth since this morning."

someone

Wade turned and ran, looking for Quinn and Kenneth. He called Quinn on the comm.

"I'm at 1. I can see out past the entrance," Quinn told him. "There're guys down there with those weird guns. They got out of a, uh, flying machine."

"How many men?" Wade asked.

"Four," she answered.

Wade heard two gunshots, one unfamiliar and the other Quinn's.

"Three," she corrected herself.

"You shot one?"

"He shot at me first. His gun is different..."

"Get downstairs!" Wade ordered. Did Terra have real guns now? "I'll be there in a couple minutes."

He pocketed the comm and pushed himself to go faster. When he arrived, he could see that the men had already made it inside. A gunshot resounded, followed by another shot from the Terrian gun. Then quiet. Wade ran to the back door and punched in the code, then again because he messed it up.

He sprinted across the cafeteria and headed into the

empty hallway. He heard a loud cry from the stairs and ran to them. He drew his pistol.

He snuck up the stairs. Quinn's gun lay on the floor; he grabbed and holstered it. He rounded a corner, and there was Quinn lying on the stairs as a man in an Enforcer uniform stomped on her left knee.

Wade took aim at the man's torso, but his gun misfired. The Enforcer kicked Quinn in the stomach, sending her sprawling, and aimed his rifle-like weapon at Wade.

Wade could tell that gun was different from the others; its long barrel was made for bullets. Terra had upped her game. Wade raised his hands. The Enforcer smirked, turning his Terrian gun and attention toward Quinn.

Wade snatched her revolver from his holster and put the Enforcer down with two shots. The man collapsed, rolling down the stairs past him.

"That was one quick draw," Quinn said. "You gotta show me how you do that without dropping it."

"Are you alright?" Wade asked, holstering the gun and hurrying up to Quinn.

"Sure," she said, grabbing the handrail and pulling herself up.

She took a step out and nearly fell down the stairs herself. There was something wrong with that left knee. Wade took her shoulders and helped her stand up straight.

"Where's the other man who was here?" he asked.

"They shot him with one of those electrical things, and he fell over the side," she told him.

Wade nodded. He picked up the Enforcer's discarded rifle.

"Let's go. There's not much time left," he told her.

They attempted walking, but that was taking too long, so Wade lifted Quinn into his arms and made his way down the stairs as quickly as he could. She grimaced in pain the whole way down. Once outside, Wade ran.

Quinn was still heavy as the dickens, but he managed to maintain a decent speed. He suddenly remembered Kenneth. They would not make it if he tried to go looking for him. He could only hope that Kenneth had made it outside. Twelve minutes later, he could see the exit. They were almost there.

The sound of the helicopters had grown steadily louder.

He could see them now; there were three. They were black, sleek, and gleaming in the sunlight. By the time Wade reached the exit, the helicopters had nearly arrived.

He could have sworn he heard another helicopter -some incongruent sound, standing out from the others- but he only saw the three. They reached the town, and paused overtop of it.

Then, he did see another helicopter. It seemed to come out of nowhere. This one was different- it was a dull green color, and bulky compared to the black ones. It looked older than them, too. He could barely see some sort of emblem on the side, and a pair of long sticklike appendages sticking out from a window.

Suddenly the things lit up. They were guns, Wade saw. Real guns, like his and Quinn's six-shooters.

"What is that?" came Quinn's voice, barely audible.

"I'm not entirely sure," Wade answered, peering up at the thing.

It was shooting at the other helicopters. A black one began spinning out of control, heading for the RT below. Rather too near for Wade's liking.

Just as the helicopter crashed, Wade made it out of the town and behind one of the outer buildings. He did not see the rest of their group, but figured them to be out of harm's way.

He set Quinn down and peeked out around the building. The large green helicopter was shooting again. It downed another of the black helicopters. This one began spinning out even more violently than the first.

The helicopter turned, facing where Wade and Quinn were hiding. A terrible noise filled Wade's ears as the helicopter crashed into the building.

Everything went blank, and when he recovered his wits he found himself pinned facedown, surrounded by near-darkness and the creaking, collapsing building.

"Quinn?" he shouted. "Quinn!"

"Here," she answered, from somewhere behind him. He twisted as far as he could to look for her. He spotted her small form, belly-crawling toward him. She came up beside him, and he grabbed the back of her jacket, pulling her the rest of the way.

"I can't move," he said.

Quinn pushed up on her elbows and tried to shove away the piece of wall pinning his lower half, but couldn't manage it in the small space. After a few minutes of straining, she settled back down beside him. They lay there in silence for a few moments. Wade could hear the structure breaking down around them. It would not last long.

"Wade?" Quinn asked.

"Yes?" he replied.

"Think we're gonna make it out of here?" she said, glancing around.

"Yeah," he said, slowly. "I do."

She paused, and he could tell she was thinking.

"Just in case," she said. "How does that prayer go again?"

"That…prayer?"

A loud crash resounded, and the ground shook. Quinn looked at him urgently as it subsided.

"I'm going wherever you're going," she said.

"It's something like this…" he began.

He took her hands and held them while she quickly repeated the words after him, her eyes squeezed shut and nose scrunched.

She opened her eyes at the end. "Amen?"

He nodded. "Amen."

The ground began shaking again, and a huge roar started up. Wade grabbed Quinn and pulled her closer, covering her head with his arm. The noise grew deafening, and the building folded over itself, enveloping them in a sea of wood, bricks, and grime.

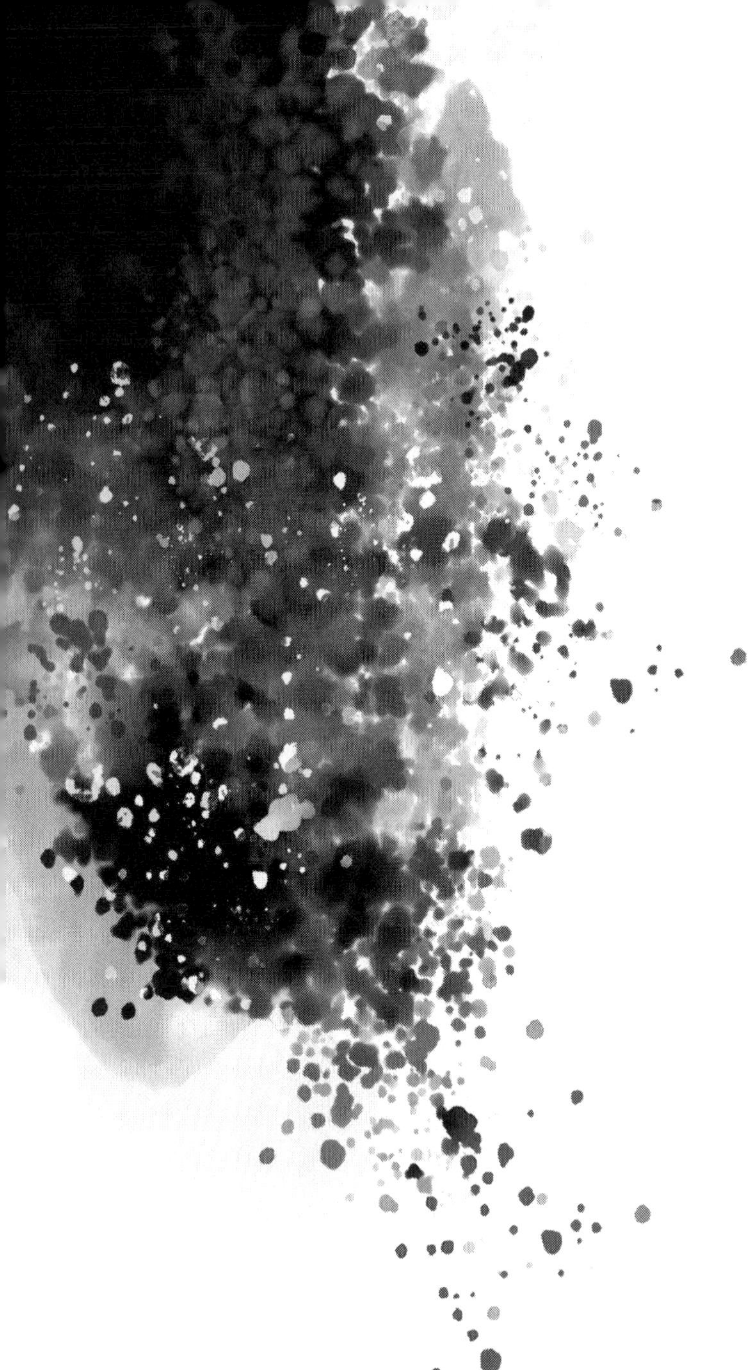

XVI

Quinn opened her eyes slowly; her lids felt heavy and there was a bright light coming from somewhere. Things looked hazy, but she could see the outline of a person across the room.

She forced her eyelids up farther and waited for her sight to adjust. She pushed up on her elbows and squinted. The man's face drifted in and out of focus, but she recognized him as Wade.

"Wade?" she said softly.

Wade stirred and opened his eyes. They fixed on hers.

"Well good morning, Missy Quinn," he said.

"Where are we?" she asked groggily. "What is this

place? What about the-"

She tried to sit up, but the motion vexed her knee terribly. Wade stood and crossed to her bedside.

"Calm down," he said. "Your knee got real jacked up."

She huffed, "No kidding."

She relaxed against the bed and looked up at him. He had a large bandage on the side of his head, and several more up and down his arms.

"What happened to your head?" she asked.

"Took a rock to it. I'm alright," he said. "Though it seems both of us were out of it for a day or so."

"What is this place?"

"This is what they're calling a hospital." He walked to the other side of the room and opened a window. Light flooded in, momentarily blinding her.

"And that out there," he said. "Is what they call Resnovas."

"Res-what?" she asked.

Outside, she could see a great blue body of water, surrounded by white sand. Further back, there was a dense line of strange trees. The colors were brighter than any she had seen before. She shook her head in wonder.

"Resnovas," Wade said again.

"What is it?"

"A rebel group. A country, really. Terra didn't know they existed, until now. They saw our message and decided now was the time to strike. That other helicopter was theirs. They brought the RT people here..."

Quinn tried to let what he was telling her sink in. It was getting sort of jumbled together in her head. Wade peered at her.

"You better go on back to sleep," he said. "All the color left your face."

She frowned, thought about arguing, but decided against it.

"Alright," she said slowly. "Just don't go anywhere, please?"

"I won't," he assured. He sat in a chair beside the cot. Quinn closed her eyes and let the haze take her back to sleep.

When Quinn woke again, Wade was as he had been, but now Addi sat beside him in another chair, her head resting on his arm. Both were asleep, both looked peaceful. She smiled.

She sat up slowly, noticing that she wore some of that strange, soft Terrian clothing. She pulled up her left pant-leg to see her knee. It was bound in a bulky black concoction of metal, fabric, and padding. She looked around, spotting her own clothes on a shelf across the room.

The room was small and plain, empty except for her bed, the couple of chairs, and the shelf. Over the door hung a small flag, and on it an emblem: a roughly painted black tree on a white background, with little flecks of red and blue sprinkled throughout its leaves.

Her mind was clearer now, and she attempted to piece together the information she could recall. She remembered being trapped under that collapsing building, and the very important conversation she'd had with Jesus just then, and hearing a terrible noise before everything went dark...

Wade's eyes opened. "You remember anything?" he whispered, getting out of his chair and sitting beside her on the bed.

She nodded, a grin pulling at her mouth. "You're stuck

with me for good now."

"Now through eternity," he said quietly. He wrapped one arm around her shoulders, and she leaned her head against his.

"Did they get everyone out?" she asked.

"Most everyone," Wade said; he frowned sadly. "Kenneth didn't make it out."

Quinn took his hand, squeezing his fingers. Addi woke up then.

"Goodness, Quinn," Addi said. "Look at that hair." She moved to the bed and sat in front of Quinn. "May I?"

"Yes," Quinn answered hesitantly, not exactly sure what she meant.

Addi gently ran her fingers through Quinn's short hair, brushing it out. Quinn closed her eyes.

"There," Addi said a couple minutes later.

"Very nice," said Wade. "I think I did pretty good on her haircut."

Addi raised her brows skeptically, looking from Quinn's rough ends to Wade.

"All I had was a hunting knife," he said.

"This is a story I must hear," Addi said. "But first. Lunch."

She stood and crossed to the door. "I will be back. Behave."

"Will you open the window?" Quinn asked, looking at Wade.

He obliged and the room was flooded with natural light. She gazed at that blue water.

"I'll take you out there," he promised.

Addi returned a few minutes later, and the three of them ate together. Afterward, Wade and Addi left to see someone about where they'd be staying.

Quinn wasn't sure how much time had passed when she heard a knock at the door.

She sat up and said, "Come in."

The door opened, and a young man walked in. He was tall and broad, and had a kind look about him. His eyes met hers, and she was struck by how green they were. Under one arm, he held two large books.

"Hello," she said, tilting her head a little.

"Hello," he replied.

someone

He offered a smile, and she offered her hand. He took it without doing the left-hand-right-hand dance.

"I'm Wyatt," he told her.

"Quinn," she said.

"I like that," he said. "I do not think I've met someone with that name before."

"Well, I reckon you're the first," she said, smiling. "Ain't ever been complimented on it."

He sat down in Wade's chair and told her just a little about himself- that he'd come to Resnovas with his toddler sister only a year ago. She sensed a story there.

He spoke the way everyone in Terra did, though he did allow himself some contractions. He was very clear and obviously not one to waste time with unnecessary talking.

She liked him already.

"Now," said Wyatt. "Let me tell you about Resnovas."

Resnovas had begun as a small group of people from a place he called the Farms; she did not want to interrupt him, so she would ask about that later. They had been slowly taking in people from Terra over many years, building their populace and organizing themselves under what he called democracy.

They had been preparing to take on Terra, but had not yet found an opportune time. He told her that they had a contact within the Terrian government who'd alerted them to the insurrection in the RT. They had seized the moment to reveal themselves.

Wyatt set the books beside her on the bed. One of them had the title "World History" and the other "Holy Bible."

"These will tell you," he said. "What came before. You'll notice a pattern." He smiled softly. "There is nothing new under the sun."

She nodded. "Thank you."

She shook his hand again, and he left the room. She lifted the World History book into her lap and opened it up to the first page. She had not yet considered what came before Terra. Now she was very curious.

She flipped through the book, skimming pages. Something caught her eye: a bright painted picture of a man on a horse, dressed like her and Wade and taking aim with a long rifle. She went back a few pages, finding the beginning of the chapter: "The American Frontier: Westward Expansion". She began reading.

The next day she was discharged from the hospital and given a Resnovian ID card. The card had her picture and name, Quinn Walker; with no known last name, she'd taken Wade's.

Wade and Addi had secured a house for the three of them. It had a small yard with a trail leading out to a small bay. Once her knee had healed and she was able to walk, she, Wade, and Addi had gone to see the blue water.

"Now that," Quinn said. "Really makes me feel like I'm on another world."

She walked out to calf-deep water, enjoying the spray on her legs and the cool wind on her neck. Down the beach, she saw a man kneeling in the sand with a little girl. She recognized them as Wyatt and his little sister whom he'd told her about. She caught his eye, smiled, and waved. He waved his sister's hand back.

Quinn returned to the shore where Wade and Addi stood, watching. Taking her place between them, they walked home together.

Notes

-Wade Walker's message takes inspiration from the words of Thomas Paine in his 1776 pamphlet, *Common Sense*. The language is intended to reflect that of the revolutionary work. Such writings have often been instrumental in the fight for freedom throughout history.

-The translation of Psalm 91 is from the 1599 Geneva Version. Derived from William Tyndale's translation and banned by King James I, it was one of the first Bibles brought to America and included study notes from early Reformation leaders. This could have helped form Wade's thinking regarding freedom and tyranny, just as it did early Americans.

THE RESNOVAS SERIES

AVAILABLE NOW

RESNOVAS | I
something
T.G. Scott

RESNOVAS | II
someone
T.G. Scott

COMING SOON

RESNOVAS
III

RESNOVAS
IV

AVAILABLE IN PAPERBACK AND EBOOK

Follow @tg_scott_writer on Instagram for book updates and BTS content!

Scan for the rest of **The Resnovas Series**:

about the author

T.G. Scott is a writer, artist, and musician from the Gulf Coast. She enjoys being outside in God's Creation, spending time with her family, and eating good food. If you were to get close enough to see her in her natural habitat, you'd probably find her shredding on her guitar, writing stories, or having a deep conversation with one of her dogs.

Someone is the second book in Scott's **Resnovas Series.**

Made in the USA
Columbia, SC
21 September 2024